Follow Your Heart

By J. B. Williams

J. B. Williams

ISBN: 978-0-6151-6185-3

PUBLISHED BY JANICE BRAUN WILLIAMS

www.janicebraunwilliams.com

Newcastle, California

Printed in the United States of America

Chapter 1

Y esterday earned the honor of the worst day of my
veterinary career thus far which isn't saying much since
I am a twenty-eight year old with only a year of experience
under my belt. Within the space of an hour, three horses with
symptoms of colic came into the clinic. X-rays showed the
cause of the horses' discomfort wasn't colic but stomach stones
the size of grapefruits that had become lodged between the large
and small intestines.

Two of the horses were candidates for surgery. The
third, a twenty-eight-year old gelding, wasn't. Peritonitis had set
in, and we had no alternative but to put him to sleep. This is the
part of veterinary medicine I hate—watching an owner say
goodbye to a loving friend. When I left the clinic last night, the
owner sat cross-legged on the floor of the stall with her dead

horse's head in her lap—a sight that is hard to forget. To dull the pain, I remind myself of happier times when I saved an animal who should have died.

That was yesterday. Today I'm sitting in a beach chair, basking in the sun. Salt air caresses my body as I close my eyes and listen to the sounds of squealing children playing in the surf. Seagulls squawk overhead as I eavesdrop on a conversation between two bronze-skinned teenage girls wearing skimpy bikinis.

"There he is," one of them sighs. "Isn't he gorgeous?"

I can't resist and sit up. On the watery horizon several surfers bob up and down in wait of the perfect wave, the one that triggers heart pounding excitement in them and in those of us who watch from the beach. My heart races when a brightly clad daredevil rises to his feet and spreads his arms for balance. Moments later he bites the big one and disappears beneath the foaming surf.

Collectively, the two girls and myself gasp, "Oh, no," and press our fingertips to our lips.

It seems forever before the surfer reappears and signals to his buddies that he is all right. Until now I don't realize how involved I am. I run my tongue around the inside of my mouth and feel the rough spot where clenched teeth had grabbed flesh.

With a sigh of relief, I lean back again and listen to the palm branches rustle overhead. That same breeze carries with it music and delicious smells from the hotel patio where a sumptuous feast is being prepared by a white-capped chef. Life can't get any better than this I tell myself as I turn my head sideways and look through dark glasses at four muscular young men playing an enthusiastic game of beach volleyball.

Then the unthinkable happens. My cell phone rings. Even though I'm not on call, I can't help but wonder if one of the horses I operated on yesterday took a turn for the worse. Every fiber of my body screams out, *let Roger handle it, he's on call today.*

I try to ignore the incessant ringing until my conscience overrules my need for a day off. Sighing with resignation, I flip the instrument open.

"Hello."

"Kayla, are you all right? You took so long to answer."

Mom's voice causes me to sit upright. She never calls on my cell phone, preferring instead to wait until evening to call my home phone so we can chat without being interrupted by a needy animal. My mouth goes dry.

"Mom, what's wrong?"

There's a long pause, and then she sobs out the awful truth. "It's Brandon. He's had another stroke. It's pretty bad, honey. I think you should come home."

Brandon is my stepfather. Next to Dad, he's the most important man in my life. For a moment my world stands still while my brain wraps around the reality of Mom's call. When I find my voice, I tell her I will be there as soon as I can.

I can't think; my brain short circuits. For the longest time I sit there staring at the ocean. Then, as if shocked by a probe, I jump up, stuff my towel in my beach bag and fold up my chair. On the way to my car, a myriad of thoughts run through my mind, the least of which is, *Not Brandon, Lord. My mom needs him.*

I call to book my flight and explain my situation to the woman on the other end of the line. She tells me they have a first class seat and asks if I want it.

"Yes, please."

To avoid the congestion around the Los Angeles Airport, I take a taxi. As usual, the terminal is bustling with people. I stand impatiently behind a couple having trouble understanding how to use the automated check-in machine. After several frustrating minutes, an airport employee comes to their aid. The elderly couple thanks her profusely, apologizes to me for the delay and then walk toward the long line of people waiting to go through security.

I have better luck with the machine. Moments later it prints out my boarding pass which I show to the man behind the counter. When he asks for identification, I stare at him, my mind elsewhere. He asks again. This time his request registers. I give him an embarrassed smile. He smiles back and waits while I search through my purse.

"It seems to have swallowed my wallet," I tell him, color burning my cheeks.

He doesn't find my humor funny, so I dig faster. Finding the object of my search, I flip open my wallet and show him my driver's license, which he scrutinizes for a long moment.

"Just two pieces?" he asks, his eyes settling on my luggage.

I nod and watch him fasten the pre-printed tag to my bags.

"Enjoy your flight," he says.

"Thank you."

I walk toward the security area where I stand in line with hundreds of other travelers. I want to scream, `Hurry up. My step-father is dying', but I don't. When I reach the security area, a balding man asks me to take off my shoes. The faces around me blur into a streak of color as I slip my feet out of loafers and put them into the gray plastic container along with my purse. The impatient guard waves me through the metal detector. On the other side, I retrieve my things from the conveyor belt and look around to see if there are any vacant chairs. There are none, so I lean against the wall and shove my feet into my shoes.

I decide to buy a crossword puzzle book to occupy my time on the long flight. When I get to my departure gate, I find a seat, settle in for the hour wait and turn to the first puzzle. After a few minutes I set the book aside. I've never been able to concentrate in an airport. Why should it be any different now? Worrying about Brandon compounds the problem. I stare at people. So many languages, so many cultures all gathered in one place. For the most part, everyone is smiling. I find myself envying the other travelers who are looking forward to their flights while I'm rushing across the country in hopes I won't be too late, that Brandon will still be alive when I get there. I close my eyes and think of the days ahead. What if Brandon dies? Following that thought, another, more frightening idea comes to mind. What will happen to Mom? And then there's my step-brother, Jared. I haven't seen him since last Christmas, then only for a few days. My mind races back in time to when we were teenagers. We had a thing for each other, but it didn't last long. Jared, nineteen at the time and a college student, was too mature for me. He had our life planned: marriage after he graduated from college, and I graduated from high school; a family right away. He gave no thought to my hopes and dreams, so I returned his fraternity pin. Looking back, it was a pretty gutsy move for a sixteen year-old girl enamored with an older man.

Upon my arrival at the airport in Missoula, I follow the other travels to the baggage claim area. From my place near the carousal, I turn around and search the sea of people spilling through the automatic doors. Relief washes over me when Jared and I make eye contact. He arrives at my side in time to retrieve my baggage. And after a quick peck to my check, he leads the way toward the exit. We are outside when he inquires about my flight.

"Long. How's your dad?"

His smile fades. He shakes his head. "He's on life support. It doesn't look good."

My heart aches for Brandon. I can't imagine him with tubes keeping him alive. I hesitate and then ask, "How do you feel about that? Is that what he would have wanted?"

Jared expels a long, low sigh. The muscles in his jaw tense. He doesn't answer my question until we are settled in the front seat of the Suburban. He starts the truck and turns to look at me. "I'm waiting for your mom. She's not ready to let go. Maybe now that you're here..." His voice drops off as tears fill his eyes. His mouth works hard to hold back his emotions.

Even though we've had our differences, it's hard to see him like this. On impulse, I reach across the space separating us and lay my hand on his. "It's all right, Jared, God is preparing a place for Brandon. Only his body will die. Mom will be all right. She's a tough lady. We'll get through this together, the three of us." I rub his hand and add, "And don't forget Uncle Frank and Aunt Sarah. They will be there for her. She'll be okay."

He nods and sniffs, and then he just stares at me for a few seconds. "If I recall, you and God weren't speaking." He manages a smile. "I see things have changed, eh?"

Color rises in my cheeks. It is one thing to admit there was a time I was angry with God—another to find out Jared knew all along.

Before backing out of the parking space, he draws his shirt sleeve across his eyes. I'm taken aback. In the past, Jared would never have allowed anyone, especially a woman, to see him cry. On the way to the hospital he tells me what to expect, but words don't prepare me for what I see when we walk into Brandon's room. Brandon's face is the color of Elmer's Glue. His hair turned gray since the last time I saw him. The walls are white; he's covered in white sheets. The only color comes from the drapes, which are a soft shade of yellow. A machine breathes for him, another relieves his body fluids. A quick look at the monitor beside the bed tells me his blood pressure is dangerously low, so is his pulse. The room smells of death, yet my mind can't grasp life without Brandon McChesney. I glance around the room for some indication Mom is in the hospital. My eyes rest on the sweater draped over the back of the only chair.

Jared touches my elbow. "She's probably gone out for a cup of coffee. Do you want to find her?"

I shake my head and move toward Brandon's bedside. I'm afraid to lift his hand in case I interfere with the intravenous tubes, so I bend over and kiss his cold, clammy forehead. I whisper his name. He doesn't respond, but then I don't expect him to. I back away and bump into Jared. In a voice just above a whisper I ask him to help me find Mom. He wraps an arm around me, and we creep out of the room, as if the slightest sound will awaken Brandon.

We find Mom in the cafeteria, a cup of coffee cradled between her hands, her head bowed as if in prayer. Our footsteps alert her to our coming. She looks up at us like we're strangers. Then, as if a light goes on, her eyes fill with recognition. She leaps to her feet and opens her arms. We hold one another for a long time before stepping apart. Seeing her like this reminds me that to love someone is to set ourselves up for a moment like this.

"It's okay, Mom. He's in God's hands," I say.

She nods and produces a tissue from her pocket. After wiping her nose, she smiles at Jared and asks if either of us has eaten anything.

"I haven't." He looks at me.

"Neither have I. They don't feed you on the plane any more."

Jared reaches for Mom's hand. "It's settled then. We'll go to Denny's. It's just down the street."

Panic fills Mom's eyes. She looks from me to him and back again. "I can't. What if..."

Jared moves closer and wraps his arm around her. "There's nothing you can do, Maggie. Besides, we need to go some place and talk. Please."

The pain in Jared's voice is palpable.

I wrap my arm around Mom's waist, just above Jared's arm and give her a squeeze. She looks up at Jared, then sideways at me. Years melt away. Mom is like a little child. She sags against me and allows us to take her out of the hospital, but not before stopping at the nurses' station to tell them where we are going.

"Call me if anything happens," she tells the nurse.

At the restaurant, Mom takes her phone from her purse and lays it on the table, right next to the salt and pepper shakers. Jared reaches across the table and takes her hands.

"We have to talk about this, Maggie. Dad wouldn't want to be kept alive. You know that."

Mom's lip quivers. She stares at their clasped hands as tears begin to roll down her cheeks. One after the other they drop to the table cloth. I can't bear her suffering and pray for words of comfort that never come. I cover their hands with mine and this is the way we are when the call comes. The three of us stare at the phone. On the fourth ring, Jared releases Mom's hands, and I take my hands off his. I draw a breath and listen as he greets the caller. He doesn't say so, but Mom and I know Brandon is gone.

Mom cries into a tissue. Other than glassy eyes, Jared sits in stoic silence while absorbing the fact his dad is now a memory. I can't speak. Brandon loved me as if I were his biological daughter. But more than that, he loved my mother very much. Everything he did, he did for her. He also made the world a better place for the less fortunate; strange how grief brings back memories. I picture Brandon in a Santa hat, the Suburban piled high with presents and bags of food.

Five hundred people come to say goodbye to Brandon McChesney. The eulogy is given by the Governor of Montana. Congressmen and judges sit amongst local townsfolk, all gathered under a cloudy sky on a hill above Brandon's beloved ranch. Jared stands behind the lectern. While composing himself, he surveys the green pastures dotted with prize winning cattle and horses. His eyes mist over. When he finally speaks, his voice quivers with emotion.

"Dad loved this ranch. That's why we chose this spot, so he can keep tabs on us," Jared says with tears in his eyes.

A masculine voice murmurs a hearty, "Amen to that."

Through a veil of tears I smile at Derek, a friend I've known since I was sixteen. Back then Derek worked for Brandon as ranch manager. We became acquainted when I decided to try women's barrel racing and he volunteered to help train my horse. Derek holds a worn Bible. He waits for Jared to sit down, and then he stands and begins to read. Halfway through the twenty-third Psalm an unexpected wind rustles through the treetops. Derek stops and smiles as if he sees something the rest of us don't.

"Happy trails, Brandon. We'll be seeing you," he says and goes on as if he hadn't been interrupted.

At the end of the service the vocalist sings Amazing Grace, the strains of which echo into the hills and back again. At the conclusion of the song, Mom places a white rose on the casket. Jared and I do the same before walking down the hill to the house. By the time we reach the patio, Mom is in control. She smiles and greets each guest before pointing them in the direction of the buffet table the ladies of the church have prepared.

Among the people in attendance are Clara and Bryan, friends of mine from my high school days. They live in New York now, so this is a bittersweet reunion. Bryan is a successful attorney practicing law in New York. They have two gorgeous kids. Now that the children are in school, Clara is back to work as a makeup artist, plying her trade on Broadway.

We hug. Fresh tears spring into my eyes. Quickly, so Mom doesn't see, I pull a tissue from my pocket and wipe away the dampness.

"He was a good man," Bryan says, the standard remark at a time like this but oh so true.

"Missoula will miss him," Clara adds.

It's hard, but I manage a token smile. "Just think, a Christmas without Brandon."

"Who will continue the tradition of delivering Christmas baskets?" Clara asks.

Without thinking, I say, "I will."

"You can count me in," a masculine voice says.

I look over my shoulder. Derek is standing there, a plate of food in his hand, a smile on his face.

"I'll hold you to that," I reply.

"I hope you will." He gives me a shy smile and shoves the food around his plate with a plastic fork. "Does that mean you'll be staying in Montana?"

I look from one face to the other. Everyone is waiting. At a time like this his boldness surprises me. "It means I will be here in plenty of time to distribute the Christmas baskets if someone will put them together. Don't read more into it than that." The words are out and I'm immediately sorry for the sharp tone of my voice.

His smile is replaced by a look of disappointment. "Sorry to hear that," he says and walks away.

I watch the easy way he communicates with people. His smile is genuine as he pats the man's shoulder. Then he turns to greet a young woman. It's obvious she is enamored with him. Her face brightens like a light bulb that's just been switched on.

Moreover, their subdued laughter makes me envious. I want to laugh too, but the pain of Brandon's death won't let me.

"They're just friends," Clara says, as if I care.

Our eyes meet—hers with understanding, mine with confusion. Until now I hadn't given much thought to a future in Montana. Nothing held me here—not really. But now that Mom is alone, I at least have to give thought to the idea.

Clara wraps her arm around me and whispers, "When the pain goes away, you might change your mind about Montana. Your Mom needs you now more than ever. And then there's Derek. He's in love with you, Kayla. Why do you think he's still single?"

I shrug off her question. The last thing I want to discuss is Derek. Rather than continue down this path, I change the topic. "So, what have you guys been up to?" I know once Clara begins talking about New York everything else is forgotten. Thirty minutes later, Clara takes a breath. Bryan and I roll our eyes and have a good chuckle at her expense.

It's not until later, when everyone has gone, I find myself walking Derek to his truck. Above us, stars look like strings of white Christmas lights wrapped around a crescent moon that hangs suspended in time and space. Before he gets into the truck, Derek turns to face me.

"I know this is a difficult time for you, Kayla, but I was wondering…maybe…do…do you think we could have dinner before you go back?"

My first impulse is to say no, but his head nods up and down like one of those silly bobble-head dolls. I can't help but laugh. "I expect we can," I tease.

Relief passes over his face. I half expect him to jump up and down and clap his hands.

"How about a week from Friday, will you still be here?" he asks.

Clara's words echo in my head. *He's in love with you, Kayla. He's been in love with you for years.* Even as the night air begins to chill, my face warms at the thought.

Maybe it's time I think about settling down. I'm not getting any younger. Look at Clara and Bryan. They've already started a family, and I'm living in an apartment with no one to come home to.

This isn't a new concept. I've been having these thoughts lately, especially when I see a young couple pushing a stroller down the street or parents playing with their toddlers in the park. It's then I realize time is running out for me.

The little voice in my head says, d*on't go jumping into a relationship, girl. There are plenty of career women out there* *who don't need a man and children to complete their lives.* But my heart says different. I want what Brandon and Mom had.

I realize Derek is still standing there, waiting. "That would be nice—dinner I mean. You did say dinner, didn't you?" The words dance around my tongue and come out all wrong. Color rushes to my face. Efforts to regain control fail. "I er…er…I don't leave until that Sunday, so Friday will be fine."

Derek nods and gets into the truck. He drives away, and I stand there for the longest time watching the taillights bounce down the driveway.

Clara could be right. Maybe Derek has feelings for me. What if he expresses those feelings? What if he asks me to stay in Montana?

I'm lost in thought when I hear a noise behind me. I spin around just in time to see Jared disappear around the corner of the house. The thought that he had been eavesdropping on a private conversation makes my blood boil. I go after him, and when I reach the back yard, I find the buffet table cleared and the women of the church gone. So is Jared. With an exasperated sigh, I vow to confront him in the morning.

J. B. Williams

Chapter 2

The following morning I dress in haste, brush my teeth and comb my hair. I pass Jared's open bedroom door on my way downstairs and lean inside. The bed is made. I continue down the hall and stop in front of Mom's open bedroom door. She's staring out the window at the fresh mound of dirt. Beneath the terry cloth robe her shoulders rise and fall with each sob. I contemplate going in, but I talk myself out of it. My rationale—everyone needs to grieve, it's a normal process that is best done alone.

The kitchen is empty and quiet, except for the gurgling sound the coffee pot makes toward the end of its cycle. By process of elimination, I assume Jared made the coffee before going to the barn. If that's the case, he'll be back. I pour a cup and sit at the kitchen table where I rehearse my lecture about listening in on a private conversation. Thirty minutes later I am still waiting. That's when the thought comes to me. He isn't coming. I down the last dregs of coffee, rinse the cup, and put it in the dishwasher. On my way out I notice Jared's truck isn't parked in its usual spot. *Where could he be this time of morning?* As happens sometimes, my mind conjures up scenarios—one of which is that he went to tell Derek to stay away from me. You can imagine my surprise when I enter the barn and see Jared. He's wearing jeans, a blue plaid western shirt and a worn cowboy hat I'm certain belonged to Brandon. Hence my theory that he went to confront Derek is shot with holes. A tiny part of me is disappointed. What a jerk I am.

When he sees me, his face brightens into a broad smile. "Good morning, I'm going for a ride. How about joining me?"

He doesn't notice the battle going on inside me. Without waiting for an answer, he hands me the reins of a chestnut gelding who is saddled and bridled.

"I'll be right back," he calls over his shoulder and walks down the barn aisle.

I stare after him, mouth agape.

What makes him think I want to spend ten minutes with him, let alone go for a ride with him?

I stifle the urge to yell after him that I'm busy. Instead, I watch his all too familiar swagger as he walks away from me.

He stops in front of the first stall, opens the door and disappears inside. Moments later he emerges leading another one of the ranch horses.

Why is it that I can't stand up to him? Maybe it's *the way he looks at me—eyes taking me in, in one fell sweep.*

He gives me a lazy smile as he passes me on his way to the grooming area, where he ties the horse to a ring mounted on the wall. "You do remember how to ride, don't you?" he asks, peering over the horse's rump.

Rather than admit I'm a bit apprehensive about riding after all these years, I ignore his comment and wait for him to groom and saddle his horse. When he is finished, he follows me as I lead my horse outside. Before mounting, I make sure the girth is tight. My stomach knots as I put a foot in the stirrup. It doesn't stay knotted long. The old adage is true—once a horseman, always a horseman—kind of like riding a bicycle, one never forgets how. I lean over to caress the silken coat of the gelding. As I do, I see Jared out of the corner of my eye. He checks his girth and reaches for the saddle horn. Agile as ever, he swings into the saddle and stares at me a long moment. Angry or not, I'm not blind. He's one attractive man, and I'm sure women drool over him—until they know him like I do.

I give him an indifferent glance. "Are you going to sit there all day?"

Either he doesn't hear or he ignores the impatient tone of my voice. "You look good on him." He waits a moment before adding, "He's your mare's first foal."

I'm certain he tells me this to put me on a guilt trip for not having stopped in to see Lady since I've been home. But I don't let him get to me. I don't tell him I haven't wanted to see her, that seeing her will bring back memories of the accident that shattered my dreams of a world-class ladies barrel racing title. Jared's eyes hold mine longer than necessary. Warning sirens go off in my head. Heat warms my cheeks. In an effort to calm my beating heart, I wrench my eyes from his and look away. I stroke the gelding's muscled neck until I'm sure I won't crumble beneath Jared's prying eyes. When I look at him again, he's smiling as if he knows the effect he has on me.

"What's his name?" I ask.

"His registered name or his barn name?"

"His barn name."

"Copper, like the color of your hair."

For a moment my insides turn to jelly. Then I'm angry because I hate what he does to me. Rather than say something I will be sorry for later, I cluck and Copper lopes off. I forgot how wonderful it is to feel the power of a horse beneath me. Wind stings my eyes as I allow Copper to gallop. Behind us I hear the hoof beats of Jared's horse. I prepare myself in case

Copper decides the race is on, but Copper isn't the least bit bothered. His easy gait remains unchanged.

We ride side by side as the landscape rushes by. Wind takes our laughter away as we gallop up the backside of the hill where Brandon is buried. At the top, we rein our horses to a halt. The joy of a few minutes ago is replaced with a mixture of sadness and reverence. Jared dismounts. Hat in hand, he walks toward his father's grave and stands quietly for several minutes. My heart breaks for him. He rearranges the flowers in a vase embedded in the headstone and then draws the sleeve of his shirt across his eyes.

As I wait, I feel Brandon's spirit in this place. It's like Jared said at the memorial service, 'a perfect place from which to keep tabs on everyone'.

Tears burn my eyes. I turn away and look down the hill toward the barn Brandon built. I find it a bit ironic that at this precise moment Derek walks out of the back of the barn. Copper whinnies, and Derek glances up at me. He waves. I wave back and settle a little deeper into the saddle and look over the green, rolling hills. As I contemplate life without Brandon, the squeak of leather alerts me. I glance over my shoulder. Jared is ready to ride on. Without a word, he turns his horse toward the narrow trail that winds its way beneath gnarled old oak trees. When we reach the bottom, he takes a single-track trail toward the sound of cascading water. I recall the first time Lady and I crossed this stream. Instead of walking into the fast moving current, she surprised me and jumped to the other side, nearly unseating me. To my delight, Lady's son isn't afraid of water. He plunges in behind Jared's horse and stops. His knees begin to buckle and I say, "Oh, no, you're not lying down with me on your back."

Jared's laughter echoes off the rocky walls on either side of the creek. The nice thing about laughter is that it's infectious. I grapple with the reins and finally pull my horse's head back up where it belongs. Once we are on the other side of the water, I laugh too.

"You should have seen your face," he says, grinning from ear to ear. "I forgot to tell you Copper loves water. If you turn him loose, he'll drop to his knees and roll upside down. He thinks he's a fish."

We both laugh and continue toward the fence line where we first met twelve years ago. If I didn't know better, I'd say Jared is trying to invoke memories. Maybe this has something to do with my dinner date with Derek. I don't have long to wait to see if this is true. When we get to the top of the hill, Jared dismounts and ties his horse to the fence. As I dismount, he wraps his hands around my waist and lowers me to the ground. Without warning, he kisses me. His lips are electrifying, almost urgent. My body trembles in his arms. I tell myself I don't want this, but my brain doesn't get the message. After a long, breathless moment, he backs away with his hands still on my waist; eyes the color of green oats stare at me from beneath the brim of his Stetson.

"Stay here and help me run the ranch. You know it's what my father wanted," he says, his voice husky and thick.

"Jared…,"

He stops my excuse with another, more passionate kiss I try to stop by placing my hands against his chest. He doesn't get the message, so I push harder. At last he loosens his grip. I'm breathless and frightened of my own desires. Tears spring into my eyes as I wriggle free. In self-defense I blurt out, "Don't do that again."

I feel color rush into my face.

He stares at me a long moment before saying, "You're afraid to let your guard down." His lips curl into a smile. He bends and pulls a piece of wild oats from the ground and chews on it as he watches me. "That's it, isn't it, Kayla? You're scared to follow your heart."

Without answering him, I turn and walk to the fence where Copper is tied. The crunch of his boots follows me. He grabs my arm and swings me around.

"I don't want you seeing Derek," he says.

My thoughts go back to when we were young, when he asked me to wear his fraternity pin. I was naive but it didn't take long to realize being pinned to Jared meant agreeing with him on everything. Standing here now, I see he hasn't changed. His need to control every situation is a flaw in his character that I can't overlook no matter how much chemistry there is between us. I draw a breath to quell my rising temper. When his fingers tighten around my arm, I pull away, yet my eyes hold his, defying him to stop me from leaving.

"Derek and I are friends. We are having dinner whether you like it or not." I yank my arm free, adding, "Don't tell me what to do. I'm not a sixteen year-old girl or haven't you noticed?"

He looks me up and down and sneers. "A man would have to be blind not to see you are every bit a grown woman." He comes closer, and I back into Copper. The gelding sidesteps away from my weight. I lose my footing, and Jared reaches out to stop me from falling beneath the horse's hooves.

I mutter, "Thank you," and untie Copper. All I want is to get as far away from him as possible in the shortest amount of time.

Jared shakes his head and chuckles.

"What's so funny?" I ask.

"You haven't changed a bit. You're still a scared little girl running from her own feelings. Go on. Have dinner with Derek. He's safe. He doesn't stir up any passion. That's what you want, isn't it, Kayla, someone safe?"

My mouth falls open. I can't believe his ego. I mount Copper, kick him into a lope and head for the back gate of the McChesney Ranch. Several minutes later I look over my shoulder. I'm surprised to see that Jared isn't following me. I'm not sure if I'm relieved or disappointed. In any case, there's no use hurrying. I rein Copper down to a walk and ponder what happened.

"Of all the egotistical, knot-headed...I can't believe he thinks he can drop into my life after twelve years."

I'm still fuming when I lead Copper into the barn. The unfortunate thing is that Derek is there, too. He pretends not to see the emotional mess I'm in. Without comment, he helps me unsaddle Copper, and when I'm finished grooming him, he offers to take the gelding back to his stall. As he walks away, he calls over his shoulder. "Pick you up at seven on Friday. Okay?"

"Perfect. See you then."

As much as I hate to admit it, Jared is right. Derek is uncomplicated. He isn't exciting. But he's as solid as the dirt beneath my feet and that goes a long way when a girl is looking for a husband or that's what I've been told.

Chapter 3

Six-thirty, Friday evening, and I'm standing in front of the closet wearing a bra and panties. My hair is in hot rollers, and I'm no closer to deciding what to wear than I was ten minutes ago. Should I wear the black sheath or the beige, sleeveless dress with matching jacket?

He'll probably wear jeans and a sports coat.

I open my mouth to call downstairs to see if Mom has something I can borrow when she calls to me from the bottom of the staircase.

"Kayla, Clara is on the phone."

The phone in my bedroom doesn't work. According to Mom, it hasn't since she caught her foot on the cord and pulled the phone off the end table a couple months ago. When I ask her why she doesn't get it fixed, she says, "I never use the phone up there, so I guess it just slipped my mind. Use mine."

I grab a robe and slip into it. Mom's bedroom is a shrine. Pictures of Brandon adorn the walls; his good Stetson and a lasso hang on the bedpost. On one of the twin dressers is a glass dish I assume Brandon must have used to hold the contents of his pockets because it's filled with odds and ends like screws, pennies, toothpicks and a small knife. Next to the dish is their wedding picture framed in silver—two smiling faces stare at me.

With my eyes fixed on the picture, I pick up the phone. "Hi, Clara, what's up?" I ask as I stare at Mom and Brandon.

"I thought you might like to join me and Bryan for dinner. We're leaving for New York in the morning."

Seeing Clara and Bryan one more time is on my list of things to do. Somehow it never got done. I'm feeling guilty that I can't accept her invitation and then it occurs to me that Derek won't mind if I ask Clara and Bryan to join us.

"Are you sure? Maybe Derek won't appreciate us crashing your date?"

"He'll understand. Besides, it's not really a date." I try way too hard to convince myself of that and Clara isn't buying it.

"Of course not," Clara replies, tongue in cheek.

"We're friends, Clara, nothing more."

"If you say so."

Arguing with Clara is like arguing with a wooden statue, so I ignore her condescending remark. "Meet us at seven at The Bridge Bistro."

I hang up before Clara gets on her marriage soap box. Back in my room, I settle on the beige dress without the jacket. I choose a simple string of pearls and matching earrings I found in Mom's jewelry box. By the time Derek arrives, I'm a nervous wreck. The doorbell rings again. One last look in the mirror, and I scurry downstairs. The house is quiet. Jared is nowhere in sight. I find that rather odd after the way he acted earlier. His absence is reason to utter a prayer of thanks. The last thing I need, or want for that matter, is for two men to make fools of themselves over me, especially since I'll be returning to California next week.

When I open the door, I'm taken aback. Derek is wearing a sports coat, slacks, shirt and a tie. I don't think I've ever seen him in anything other than a pair of jeans and a western shirt. On special occasions, he wears a sports coat over his western shirt. My gaze lingers on his face a moment longer than necessary. His dark hair, longer than I recall him wearing it, curls around his collar. I expect it's the look on my face that causes him to try to hide a smile, but he's not doing a very good job of it.

Before closing the door behind us I call out, "We're leaving, Mom."

"Have a good time," she yells from the kitchen.

Derek looks over my shoulder, down the hallway. Tiny lines of concern furrow his brow. "How's she doing? It must be tough."

I wait to answer until we are outside walking toward his car, which is parked at the end of the sidewalk. "Not very well. Maybe I'll take some more time off—suggest to Mom we take a vacation. What do you think?"

I'm as shocked as Derek. I can't imagine where this thought came from. *I can't take more time off work.* And even if I could, I don't want to. I miss the gratification of saving a patient. I even miss the long hours, but I don't tell Derek this.

"Where would you go?" he asks.

I don't know why, but I keep up the pretense even though I know it's not going to happen. "Mom's never seen Yosemite."

I glance at him, and he smiles. My brain may have forgotten but my heart hasn't. It does a little tap dance while remembering what it feels like to have his lips pressed against mine, if only for a second before Derek realized what he had done. It happened so long ago, after I'd won the championship buckle at the Cow Palace.

Derek opens the door for me and thinks aloud. "Yosemite is a very spiritual place, at least for me."

"You've been there?"

Derek shuts the door and goes around to the other side of the car. He slides in and gives me a disarming smile. "Yes, several times." There's a longing in his voice that says he needs to go back. "Bridal Veil is beautiful. I love the sheer walls of El Capitan, and there's nothing quite like climbing the back side of Half Dome." His eyes crinkle at the corners when he smiles. "You should do it—take your mom to Yosemite, I mean."

I don't recall Derek being religious, yet there's a Bible tucked in between the bucket seats. My mind goes back to a conversation we had many years ago when he confided in me about his son who was born out of wedlock. I can still see his face when he told me his ex-girlfriend moved to California to hide her pregnancy, which made it difficult for him to be there for the birth of his son.

Derek closes the car door. In this close proximity, the familiar scent of Stetson wafts past my nose. Out of the corner of my eye, I watch his slender fingers turn the key in the ignition. A tiny thrill runs up my spine when the powerful motor of the late-model Mustang comes to life with a loud rumble. When we are out of the driveway, I turn sideways in my seat to stare at his profile. He feels my gaze and takes his eyes off the road and gives me a hesitant smile.

"What?" he asks.

"You're different."

His grin widens. "How so?"

"For one thing, all these years I pictured you as a pickup man and here we are riding in a Mustang."

He gives me a mischievous smile. "Ah, ha, you have thought about me now and again." His look turns serious. "I'm not the only one who has changed. Look at you, an up and coming veterinary surgeon." He returns his attention to the on-coming cars. Even so, I get the feeling he is remembering our past as I have done the last few days. When he looks at me again, he says, "We had a lot of good times on the rodeo circuit, didn't we?"

The heat begins at the base of my throat and rises into my cheeks. I turn my head and look out the window until the beat of my heart slows to a more normal rhythm.

On an exhale, I say, "Yes, we did."

We travel in silence until I remember Clara and Bryan. I sit up a bit straighter and blurt out, "I hope you don't mind, but I invited Clara and Bryan to join us."

The energy in the air around us fizzles like a dud firecracker. I open my mouth to explain, but he speaks first.

"I was hoping to have you to myself, but I understand."

It's not what he says, but the way he says it that causes color to rush into my cheeks. You would think I'd be able to control my emotions. After all, I'm a few months shy of my twenty-ninth birthday. Without thinking, I reach out and touch his forearm. Electrical impulses dance between us. I try to speak, but the inside of my mouth feels like someone stuffed cotton in it. When I do speak, the words sound hollow and meaningless.

"I'm sorry. I should have checked with you first. I didn't know it was their last night when I accepted your invitation to dinner."

As always, Derek is a gentleman. He takes his eyes off the road and flashes me a devilish smile that sets my heart dancing. "Maybe they'll want to call it an early night. Think so?"

Instead of turning away, I flutter my lashes and fan my face with my hand. In my best southern accent I say, "Why, Mr. Anderson, I do say you're being rather bold this evening."

He chuckles, and we fall into easy conversation. Derek asks all the right questions to make me feel important. It occurs to me that this is a side of him I never knew, or maybe I was too young to appreciate him.

"You're so different," I say, as if I haven't said it before.

He turns and smiles. "You keep saying that. Explain, please."

I let out a breath and compare the old Derek with the new one. "You're more confident. Yes, that's it. And you're so peaceful. Last time I was here...."

"Last time you were here I was still blaming myself for not being able to see my son." He looks at me again, long and hard. "It takes two to ruin a relationship. I learned that from counseling."

My mouth forms a perfect 'O'. When I recover from hearing that Derek, a macho cowboy, admitted to needing help, I say, "You went to counseling?"

Derek nods. "Yeah, hard to believe isn't it? There's this group at church. They're all in different stages of grief or anger over a loss. Doesn't matter if they lost someone to death or divorce, they're grieving just the same."

I'm shocked by Derek's admission. I don't know many men who would admit to needing counseling. My interest is peeked. "How did you find out about the group?"

"From a girl I was interested in. When I asked her out, she said I had too much baggage for her to handle. She told me where the group met. That was five years ago. Now I'm one of the volunteer counselors, and I'm studying for the ministry."

My brain sends out warning signals, but my heart doesn't listen. Whether I admit it or not, I'm in the market for a husband and Derek meets all the requirements. It doesn't help that my friend, Sherry, got married and produced this adorable, blond-headed baby boy. Then they asked me to be the baby's godmother. At first I wanted to refuse, but something inside me said this might be the only chance I get to lay claim to something so wonderful and innocent. Baby Travis is the one bright spot in my otherwise ordinary existence. Every other Saturday night, without fail, Sherry and Frank drop Travis off at my apartment so they can have a 'date night'. It's a win-win situation for everyone concerned. I get to spoil Travis, his parents have a night out, and I don't have the day-to-day obligation of providing for a child.

Derek stares at me in confusion.

"Where have you been?" he asks.

Embarrassment warms my face. "Sorry, I was daydreaming."

"It's night, remember?"

"Okay, I was night dreaming. Is that better?"

I'm not sure where my hostility comes from or why I snapped at him. He frowns at me and let's the matter drop. The quietness between us goes on too long. I feel like an idiot and try to think of something neutral to talk about. Then my eyes fall on the Bible between our seats.

"Religion seems to play a big roll in your life now. When did that happen?"

Derek turns the radio down. I can tell by the smile he gives me that he's been waiting for me to ask.

"When I realized I couldn't handle life on my own, that was the first step." He pauses and takes a breath. "I needed someone to be there for me no matter what. God fills that need." He takes his eyes off the road for a minute and looks at me. "I was on my way to California to see my son when a snow storm forced me to stay the night in a hotel room. I couldn't find anything on television, so I opened the desk drawer to find the hotel menu. I found a Bible instead, placed there by the Knights of Columbus. I was ripe for the harvest, as Pastor John puts it."

He sighs and continues. "I flipped through the Bible and came upon the story of the crucifixion. Words I'd heard many times before took root. I came to the realization that Jesus died that horrible death for me so that I could have a relationship with God. I was humbled to the point I had no choice but to drop to my knees and invite Him to be the captain of my life." He turns to me again, his face bathed in the light of the rising moon. "If the Lord will have me, I want to be a minister, Kayla."

J. B. Williams

Chapter 4

Derek's confession of faith is with me all through dinner. In fact, I find it difficult to think of anything else. More than once Clara asks if something is wrong. I shake my head and pretend to be interested when she regales us with yet another story of a persnickety Broadway star.

After dinner, we say goodbye to Bryan and Clara and promise to keep in touch.

"That was nice," Derek says as he slips into the car beside me.

"Yes, it was. I miss those guys."

"You seemed a bit preoccupied. Is something bothering you?" he asks.

I shake my head and he starts the car. On the way home, I ponder the reasons why I fell away from the church. At the top of the list, the injury that kept me from living my youthful dream. And then there was the death of my best friend Hunter. He died of complications from the AIDS virus. In both cases, I prayed for a miraculous healing that never took place. After that, I found it difficult to believe in a God who allowed such a horrible disease to take Hunter away from me. What kind of God snatches away the dreams of a young girl? Forgotten feelings resurface. Through a blur of tears I stare at the white line in the middle of the road. For me it symbolizes my life— going somewhere, but where? I'm lost.

You're not lost. I've been with you. Where you are, I am.

The thought is so real, so audible that I turn my head to see if Derek hears it too, but he's watching the road, not me.

I am with you always, even unto the ends of the earth.

I swing around in my seat and stare at Derek. The uncertainty of what just occurred causes the words to tumble out over my tongue.

"Did…did…did you hear that?"

Derek glances sideways and raises a quizzical brow. "Hear what?"

Of course he didn't hear anything. There wasn't anything to hear.

Derek sees my confusion. He pulls the car over to the side of the road and reaches for my hand. I burst into tears.

Moments later I'm in his arms, face buried in his muscular chest, sobbing uncontrollably against his sports coat which becomes wet with my tears. Derek doesn't seem to mind. He rubs my back and whispers, "Everything will be all right, Kayla. Let it all out. I'm here for you."

For the next hour I unload my excess baggage. I confess to Derek my anger at God for not healing Hunter. He nods as if he understands my disappointment and encourages me to go on with a gentle squeeze to my hand.

"I didn't know it then, but I'm certain now that I was in love with Hunter. I only realized it after his death." Fresh tears spill down my cheeks, onto my dress. I look up at him and draw the back of my hand across my wet cheek. "I feel so bad that Hunter didn't know …"

Derek pushes the hair from my face and looks into my eyes. "Of course he knew you loved him. No matter what you women think, men aren't complete idiots. Besides, you're as transparent as glass or didn't you know that?"

I pretend to take exception to his comment. "Transparent?"

Derek nods and smiles. "As glass."

Before I have time to respond, he lowers his lips to mine. For a moment I freeze. As I become aware of what is happening, I realize something. This isn't the right time. I'm vulnerable, having just poured out my soul to him. I move closer to the passenger side window and turn to face him.

"Derek, please. I'm not ready for a relationship. Not yet anyway."

Disappointment fills his face. He slides back behind the wheel. Ten minutes later he pulls the Mustang to a stop in front of the house. As I search for the right words to explain my earlier behavior, Derek gets out and walks around to my side of the car. He opens the door and reaches a hand inside to help me out. Before I can tell him I'm sorry, the front door swings open. Jared stands there, bathed in a bright light. His cordial, "I thought I heard a car drive up," adds to the uneasiness between Derek and me.

Derek mumbles a polite, "Good night," and turns on his heel.

He's down the sidewalk before I find my voice.

"I had a good time," I call after him.

Either he didn't hear me or he chose not to. A moment later the powerful car roars to life, leaving Jared and me to stare after him in dismay.

"So, what's eating him?" Jared asks.

Every nerve in my body reacts. "Who says there's anything bothering him?" I give him a look cold enough to freeze dry ice and brush past him on my way upstairs. Before going to my bedroom, I glance over my shoulder. Jared is slack jawed. To drive the point home, I add another uncalled for comment. "Next time mind your own business."

Venting at Jared doesn't make me feel better. Actually, I feel worse. Inside my bedroom, I let it all out. From the depths of my being, loss, disappointment, and heartache surface— events I buried in the deepest places of my heart make themselves known. Broken beyond words, I drop to my knees and press my face against the mattress to muffle my weeping. I grieve the loss of Hunter and more recently, Brandon. I voice my thoughts aloud to God—angry accusations that He took Hunter before he had a chance to make a difference, before we had an opportunity to make a commitment to each other. I remind Him of my dream to win a women's barrel racing championship. I'm rambling on when a knock at my bedroom door interrupts my angry conversation with God. Thinking I disturbed Mom, I jump to my feet and wipe away my tears. When I open the door, Jared is there.

He clears his throat and says, "Do you want to talk about what's bothering you?"

I draw the back of my hand across my face and say, "Not really. Besides, there's too much. It would take all night."

His facial expression softens into a smile. He reaches for my hand and draws me into the hallway, toward the stairs. In the kitchen, he makes a pot of tea while I sit at the table watching. All this he does without a word. Once the tea is ready, he fills two cups, adds milk and brings the cups to the table. This is a side of Jared I haven't seen before—a softer side that takes me by surprise.

"I'm such a fool," I blurt out.

Tears splash down my face onto the kitchen tablecloth. He reaches for a napkin and hands it to me while hiding a smile behind his other hand.

"It's not funny," I scold.

He turns serious, if only for a minute. "Of course it isn't, not to you anyway. But from my side of the table it is." He leans toward me and traces his thumb down my cheek. "Your mascara is running."

Any other time I might be embarrassed. But there are other, more important things than looking like Frankenstein's Bride. Besides, I don't care what I look like, serves him right for getting involved.

"I can't do anything right," I tell him.

The slightest hint of a smile threatens to erase the serious look on his face. I glare at him, and the smile disappears. "Oh, I don't think you should go that far."

"Don't be insolent, not at a time like this."

Jared leans back with his hands behind his head. He studies me for several seconds. "I'm not being insolent. I'm being truthful. You've always been too hard on yourself. Give yourself a break, Kayla. You've been on an emotional roller coaster the past few days, and if that dim-witted guy can't understand that, too bad."

My first thought is: *Where did Jared go? Who is this guy?*

Color rises in his cheeks. Unlike the Jared I know, this man is fumbling for the right words. Seconds pass. Then he says in a husky voice, "I'm sorry I pressed you the other day. It was way too soon. I know that now. But I'm not sorry I said I love you."

Jared's eyes cloud with emotion. There was a time I returned his affection. I recall the emotional highs and lows of a sixteen year-old girl infatuated with an older man. I tell myself there's too much baggage between us. Because I don't or won't confront these old feelings, I push my chair from the table and stand.

I make eye contact with him and manage to smile. "Thanks for the tea." In the doorway I turn around. He's still sitting at the table, his back toward me. "Thanks for caring, Jared, but there's nothing you can do to make things better. See you in the morning."

The following morning I stumble into the kitchen after a restless night. Half awake, I stop in the open doorway. Instead of Mom preparing breakfast, Jared is standing in front of the stove fluffing scrambled eggs with a fork. Bacon cooks in the microwave, the aroma of fresh brewed coffee wafts through the air. On the table is a vase filled with fresh flowers cut from the garden. Until now I don't think about my attire—silk pajamas and fuzzy slippers. My hair is a mass of auburn curls that couldn't be tamed by a brush. Jared glances sideways. A bemused look passes across his face and disappears quickly.

"Good morning," he says and turns his attention to the eggs.

I run my fingers through my hair but the end result is no better. With an exasperated sigh, I concede that nothing will help short of a miracle. Jared looks at me out of the corner of his eye. On my way to the coffee pot I give him a withering glance he ignores. I pour a cup of coffee add cream and lean against the counter, legs crossed at the ankles. My eyes follow his every move from the refrigerator to the stove and then back to the refrigerator, and then to the table where he places a platter of bacon and scrambled eggs next to the vase of flowers. He brushes past me to get glasses from the cupboard. On his way back to the table he stops at the refrigerator to retrieve the orange juice. I feel a smile coming on as I watch him fill the glasses and return the carton of orange juice to its place beside the milk on the door shelf.

About this time Mom wanders in looking pensive. She's wearing yellow pajamas and a matching robe and slippers. While pouring a cup of coffee she inquires about my dinner date, not that she's really interested. Mom hasn't shown much interest in anything since Brandon passed. She takes a seat and cradles the cup in her hands.

"This is like old times," she says with a faraway look in her eyes. "I remember when the two of you argued over breakfast. Sometimes you didn't say anything—one of those silent wars." She raises a suspicious brow and asks, "Are we having one of those mornings now?"

We answer in unison. "No."

"Good, because I have something to discuss with the two of you."

She waits for us to take a seat before dropping a bombshell that renders Jared and me speechless.

"I've decided to go to the mission field in Romania with some of the ladies from our church."

Jared's eyes widen with concern. When he finally finds his voice, he says, "It's too soon, Maggie, give yourself more time."

"It's something I felt I'd like to do when I first heard about it, but of course Brandon was my life then. Now that he's gone and I'm alone…" Mom holds back tears. "You know what I mean. Now that Brandon's gone I have a lot of free time on my hands."

I see the look in Mom's eyes and remember all too well how stubborn she can be when she has her mind set on something, so I try the softer approach.

"Instead of going to Romania, why not come back to California with me. You can visit all your old friends." Reaching across the table, I lay my hand on hers. "If I can get some time off, we can go to Yosemite, just the two of us. How does that sound?"

Mom slides her hand from beneath mine and lifts her chin just a little, a sign she's not falling for my tactics. She pats my hand like she did when I was a little girl and says, "That sounds like a lovely plan, but, no. I've already talked with Doris Siders. She's bringing all the information over tomorrow morning. My passport is current, so there should be no delays."

Chapter 5

That evening after dinner Mom shows me and Jared pictures of two children she and Brandon had been planning to visit at the Romanian orphanage. Her eyes fill with tears as she speaks about the over-crowded conditions. Even though it takes me longer than Jared, I finally get the message. Mom is going to Romania with or without our approval. I settle back in my chair and listen to vivid descriptions of the children. She hands me letters written by them. I read them and begin to see why I can't talk Mom out of this trip. I'm further convinced of her determination when I learn that Brandon had wanted to share their wealth to improve the orphanage's day-to-day living conditions.

Mom looks at Jared. "This trip was planned long before your father died. It was his vision before mine ..." Her voice trails off. She sniffs back tears and takes a deep breath. "Your father was a generous, loving man. When the missionaries visited our church, they showed a video during Sunday evening service. The plight of the children touched your father's heart." The sadness in her eyes leaves momentarily, replaced by a teary smile. "He kept me awake that night talking about how God had blessed us so much that he wanted to share those blessing with the kids."

Mom's desire to complete Brandon's dream grabs me. I'm caught up in the cause. Leaning forward, eager to absorb every detail, I realize my heart longs to do something important with my life too. Not that veterinary medicine is unimportant, but something beyond working with animals.

Later, on my way upstairs, I pass Mom's open bedroom door. A frown furrows her brow as she sorts through piles of clothing. I hesitate before knocking. "Can I come in?"

She looks up and nods. "Of course, but if you're here to try to change my mind, forget it." I sit on the bed and watch her. Several minutes later she looks sideways at me. "What is it? Something is bothering you, and it's not my trip to Romania."

A big sigh climbs the steep stairs from the basement of my soul. "I wish I had something important to do—something to look forward to."

She chuckles at my soulful expression, tosses the tank top aside and pulls me into her arms. How ironic is this? Instead of me comforting her, she consoles me. For a moment I'm a little girl lost in her mother's arms. I snuggle into the warmth of Mom's body and bury my face in her hair. The scent of lilac shampoo fills my senses. She rocks me gently and whispers, "Your time will come. One day, when the time is right, God will call you to a higher cause, my darling. In the meantime, He wants you to work at the veterinary clinic. Animals are important to Him too." She leans back and brushes a hair from my face. "Maybe your higher calling is marriage and children. Have you given thought to that?" She waits. When I don't answer, she says, "I'd like grandchildren before I'm too old to enjoy them. Is that so wrong?"

I shake my head and remind her that a husband is necessary for this to happen, to which she responds, "God has someone for you, Kayla. Listen for the sound of His voice, and He'll show you who it is."

I'm close to tears. Not since Hunter have I allowed myself to feel anything for a man or to think about marriage and kids. I get up and walk to the window. The old anger resurfaces.

Why did you take him away, God? We would have been so good together. Talk to me, I'm listening. Why Hunter when there were so many bad people on earth you could have taken instead?

The silence disappoints. No words of wisdom from God again.

"Why is it that God speaks to everyone but me?" I ask.

Mom walks up behind me and wraps me in her arms, clenching her fingers together at my waist. Then, resting her chin on my shoulder, the two of us stare at Brandon's grave.

"I loved him a lot, you know. But there was a time in my life when I wasn't listening to God at all. I ran away from Brandon. I didn't want to be a ranch wife. I wanted to be an actress."

"You ran away to Hollywood," I say, continuing the story.

Mom nods. I feel the pressure of her chin digging into my shoulder. Without looking, I know her eyes are clouded with tears. Mine are too. She sniffs and reminds me if she hadn't gone to Hollywood I wouldn't be here today.

"And I did love your father…just not the way I loved Brandon. Your Dad and I were more like friends, still are for that matter. Now, dry your tears." She turns me around and makes a silly face at me. I laugh and make a face at her. The uneasiness I felt earlier is gone and it feels good.

We are still laughing when Jared appears in the doorway. His face creases with confusion. "Is everything all right?"

"Absolutely." Mom turns me loose. She tidies her hair and returns to the bed to fold a pair of slacks.

Jared comes in and wanders around the room, stopping to look at Mom and Brandon's wedding picture. My eyes follow him as he moves on, stopping again at the highboy dresser. His fingers touch Brandon's things—silver money clip, belt buckle, wallet. Everything as Brandon left it the night he went to the barn to do some accounting. When Jared turns around, our eyes meet. For a moment I'm sixteen, standing on a hill, the wind blowing through my hair. I see a tall, handsome cowboy holding the reins of a chestnut colored horse. His eyes are the color of green oats. My heart stutters. I draw a breath and remind myself we cannot be more than what we are.

You're too controlling, Jared. You rob me of who I am. There's no future for us?

Mom witnesses this silent conversation. She looks from me to Jared and back at me. I wonder what she's thinking. There was a time she opposed a romantic relationship between us, but looking at her now, I see hope in her eyes.

Oh, no, we are not you and Brandon. We aren't good together. We're like water and oil, day and night.

"I'll leave you to your packing," I mutter and leave the room. On the way down the hall, I hear Mom tell Jared I'm tired in an effort to explain my quick departure.

I'm up before sunrise, packed and ready to leave for the airport even though my flight doesn't depart until two o'clock. When Mom asks, I decline the invitation to join her and Jared for church services. As soon as they are gone, I stroll down to the barn. Lady calls out a greeting that includes multiple tosses of her head. She is telling me she is tired of being cooped up in the twelve by twelve stall. My first inclination is to turn her loose to run in the arena, but it's such a beautiful day I decide to saddle up and go for a ride. I take a long time grooming her, running my hands down her glossy coat, feeling the muscles beneath her skin. I press my face into her long, luxurious mane and inhale.

"I miss you," I tell her as I stroke her neck. Tears burn my eyes. Stupid, childish, I tell myself while putting the saddle on her back. I make quick work of cinching the girth and then lead her down the aisle and out into the bright sunlight. With a reassuring pat to her neck, I swing up into the saddle and look off into the distance. "How about it, do you want to find Ebony and his girlfriends?" I ask and Lady answers me with a deep rumble.

As we ride along, I think about Ebony, the Angus bull Jared gave me twelve years ago as a Christmas present. The bull was a few week old and orphaned when his mother rejected him. My lips curl upward as I recall how cute he looked with a red bow tied around his neck, his dark, luminous eyes staring at me in the headlights of Jared's truck. I wonder if he will recognize me.

A gentle breeze rustles through the trees. Overhead, the sky is a vivid blue, dotted with a handful of fluffy white clouds. Fresh air fills my nostrils and gets under Lady's tail. She prances and pulls on the reins. Then, snorting, she kicks out with her hind legs. I remember the thrill of her speed around the barrels. Before I lose my nerve, I relinquish control and let her go. We're off, running full speed up the dirt road, the wind stinging my eyes. In the distance, cattle call to one another. A few minutes later I pull Lady to a stop on a hill overlooking a green valley where a thousand head of Black Angus cattle graze. As I sit there, the thought comes to me that there isn't anything prettier than the McChesney Ranch.

Beneath me, Lady's body trembles as she gulps air to refill her lungs. Her neck glistens with sweat. Together we look at Brandon's heaven on earth, and for a moment I hear him whisper to me in the wind.

This is your home, Kayla. You belong here. Your mother needs you even if she says different.

"But I have my work at the clinic...," I murmur on a sigh.

Work at a clinic here in Montana.

Nudging Lady forward on the cattle path, I push the unbidden thoughts aside. As we draw closer, Ebony raises his head. He watches us for a few minutes and then goes back to munching wild oats. Lady and I circle the herd. The closer we get, the more irritated Ebony becomes. He trots toward us and stops thirty feet away. He snorts a warning. Undaunted, Lady takes a couple steps toward the bull. Ebony seems to have forgotten their friendship. He lowers his head and paws the ground. Fear constricts my breathing. Rather than wait around to find out if the bull means business, I turn Lady toward home.

"Okay, we're leaving," I say.

We canter up the hill. By the time we arrive at the barn, I'm having second thoughts about leaving before Mom goes to Romania. I mull over my options while I unsaddle Lady.

Call the clinic. You still have another week's vacation.

I'm still undecided when I walk into the kitchen. I'm surprised to see Jared standing by the refrigerator drinking a glass of milk. My eyes veer to the clock on the wall. It's after eleven. He smiles at me. "You better get a move on or you'll miss your plane."

I hate it when he tells me what to do. His comment aggravates me just enough to bring out my stubborn streak.

"I've decided to stay until after Mom leaves." I pass through the kitchen and head upstairs.

He mumbles something I ignore.

I find Mom in her room, sitting on her bed, a pile of pictures on her lap.

"When did you get home from church?"

She raises her eyes to meet mine. Her face softens. "Twenty minutes ago. Did you enjoy your ride?"

"How'd you know I went for a ride?" I ask and walk into the room.

"Jared and I saw you and Lady on the hill when we drove up."

"Oh."

Her suitcase is open. Pictures of the children in Romania lay atop her clothes. Their happy faces smile at me as I draw in a long breath. "I've decided to stay until after you leave."

Mom isn't the least surprised. She doesn't bring up the subject of an unused ticket or the wasted money. Instead, she wraps me in a warm embrace.

A week later, Jared and I take Mom to the airport. The lines are long going through security, so she insists that we leave her.

"The two of you act as if I haven't flown overseas before. Goodness sakes, I'm an adult. Go on. There's work to be done at the ranch."

Rather than argue, Jared and I kiss her goodbye and say all the appropriate things like, "travel safe, call us when you get there." As we walk toward the elevator, Mom's voice rings out. "I love you guys."

I haven't told anyone, especially Mom, but I'm petrified God will take another person I love. For the past week, I've had nightmares about Mom's plane crashing. I hear screams and ripping metal and then everything goes black, and I wake up in a cold sweat, sobbing.

The ride back home is quiet, probably because I've been such a pain that Jared doesn't know what to say, so he says nothing. He covers the silence by tuning the radio to a Christian radio station. The words to *How Great is Our God* fill my heart with a peace I haven't known for some time. I lean back against the headrest and close my eyes and meditate on the lyrics.

When we get home, Jared leaves me in the foyer. Half way up the stairs he calls down. "I have to hurry. Derek and some of the neighbors are out in the back pasture branding and giving shots."

I'm surprised to hear that Jared and Derek are working together given the fact they aren't comfortable in the same room. I turn away and walk into the den where I sink into the chair next to the fireplace. The minute I close my eyes, the enemy invades my thoughts and I begin to worry about Mom's flight. Rather than dwell on my fear, I reach for the stack of books on the side table. I'm surprised to find Brandon's Bible among them. My fingers caress the worn leather with his name embossed on the cover. I know it's silly, but I swear I can smell his aftershave. A bookmark sticks out, and I open the Bible to reveal passages highlighted in yellow.

Psalm: 23, why am I not surprised? Brandon understood what it was like to be a shepherd—maybe not to sheep, but to large herds of cattle and to a blended family. He cared for his neighbors and the less fortunate. He lived The Word in every sense. And I know that if he were on the plane with Mom, he wouldn't be afraid.

I begin to read the Psalm. Comfort warms me like the afternoon sun. I don't know why I didn't see it before, or maybe I did and I pushed it to the far corners of my heart. God loves me. He is my shepherd, and the job of a shepherd is to watch over his flock and defend it against all harm. I'm deep in thought when the back door slams shut. In a flash, I'm out of the chair, racing down the hallway toward the kitchen. At the back door I exchange my tennis shoes for riding boots and grab a jacket on the way out. When I arrive in the barn, Jared is leading one of the ranch horses out of a stall. I grab Lady's halter and open her stall door. She looks at me as if to say, 'two rides in one day is not in my contract'. I slip the halter over her muzzle, pull the leather strap over her head and secure it in the buckle. As I do, Jared gives me a lopsided grin. My heart reacts with a heavy thump. No words are shared between us, but we both know we are happy to have each other's company on such a beautiful day.

Chapter 6

We are like two kids rushing to see who can saddle their horse first. Jared wins by a few seconds. He leads his mount down the aisle toward the sunlit opening with Lady and me following him. Outside the barn, we mount up and turn our horses toward the back pasture. Once we are clear of the gate, Jared latches it to make sure the cattle don't escape. With the agility of a gymnast, he swings up into the saddle, gathers up his reins and sends his horse forward. We gallop side by side, the breeze blowing in our faces. There's nothing quite like riding a thousand pounds of muscled horse to get your adrenalin going. My heart is racing as I bend low over Lady's neck and lace my fingers through her mane for added security. The race is on. Lady inches her nose ahead of Jared's horse. Not to be outdone, the roan lunges ahead of Lady. Our laughter rides the wind. Breathless, I glance sideways in time to see him spur his mount. Lady gathers speed but age causes her to loose ground to the younger horse who gallops away with ease. Jared looks over his shoulder and his smile fades into concern. He slows his horse down on a rise overlooking a meadow where our horses take in huge gulps of air. Lady's body trembles beneath me as she stares at the activity directly below us. Cowboys on horseback are busy separating cattle into groups, herding them into make-shift corrals. Near the operation is a van used in place of the old chuck wagon seen in western movies.

Some things never change. The cowboys will sleep in bedrolls next to an open fire tonight. They'll drink lots of coffee and stay up into the wee hours sharing tales of previous round-ups, some true and some fabrications of creative minds. In the morning, they will wake up to the smell of bacon frying over an open fire.

"So, how long do you think it will take?" I ask.

"A couple weeks, maybe more. Depends on how long it takes to round up the cattle in the other pastures. At last count we had a couple thousand head."

On a sigh of contentment I say, "I forgot how much I enjoy ranch life."

Jared turns sideways and gives me a hard look. The brim of his Stetson hides his eyes, so I'm not sure what he's thinking.

"Then why are you leaving?" he asks, tipping his hat back with a fingertip. Green eyes framed in tiny lines hold mine.

The fact he still knows how to light my fuse infuriates me. Rather than spar with him, I look for something safe to focus on. "I have a veterinary practice, remember?"

He doesn't acknowledge my reply. Instead, he points his horse toward the trail that meanders down into the meadow. As we ride, his words are carried back to me on a brisk breeze.

"That's all well and good, but you're needed here. Having a vet on the property is invaluable, especially during calving, and when the mares foal." Jared gives me time to ponder that statement before adding, "We're spending way too much on vet bills when we have one in the family."

What he doesn't say is that Brandon paid for my education.

We ride down the hill and arrive just as the men break for lunch. Jared dismounts and removes the bridle, replacing it with a rope halter and lead rope which ties to the picket line. While I tend to Lady he walks to the van and gets in line behind Derek. From there he watches me remove Lady's bridle, halter her and tie her alongside the other ranch horses. I offer her a bucket of water and then join the men.

Derek gives me a cursory, "Hello," before turning his attention to the table of food. I hear him say to no one in particular, "I could eat a horse. Looks good, Joe."

It never ceases to amaze me. I have a hard time putting together a decent meal in a well-equipped kitchen, but Joe manages to put on a smorgasbord of roast beef, pan fried potatoes, chili beans and corn bread using a propane stove and griddle. Not that he has to, but Joe always makes cowboy coffee over an open fire pit. It's more tradition than necessity because one look in the van tells you he brought a generator, an electric coffee pot and all sorts of modern conveniences, including a microwave oven, should the need arise. Huge ice chests hold a variety of sodas and juices.

Before filling my plate, I gaze at the sun burnt hills rising up on all sides of us. Overhead, the sky is a mixture of blue and white. The odor of cattle comes from the warm soil. My heart gives a little jolt at the sight of Ebony standing in an old wooden corral a hundred yards away. He's bellowing for his ladies while pacing the fence in search of a weak spot. On more than one occasion I've seen a bull jump an eight foot fence to get back to the herd. In this instance, the holding pen is small, so he can't get up enough speed to jump. In years past, I don't recall penning up the herd sire.

"So, what's up?" I ask Jared and Derek as I sit beside them on the ground.

They both look up from their plates with blank stares.

"Ebony, why's he penned up?"

Derek chuckles and nods to one of the cowboys sitting a few feet away. He looks a little worse for wear—hat misshapen, large bandage on his cheek, and a rip in his jeans the size of a saucer.

"Your bull's getting ornery in his old age. He went after Jess and his horse. The horse took one look at the head of steam building in that old bull and tossed Jess to Ebony as a peace offering."

Every cowboy within hearing distance laughs at the mental picture drawn by Derek. But Jess isn't laughing. He's shaking his head, muttering unkind things about Ebony that a woman can't repeat. The levity lasts the rest of lunch hour. Cowboys nudge each other and tease Jess. Jess mumbles responses that trigger more teasing, all in good fun of course. By the time the men are finished eating it is one thirty. Derek is the first to stand up, which signals the end of the lunch hour. Men grumble that their bellies are full. Derek comes back with a warning that maybe he should tell Joe not to be so creative.

"Sandwiches are fine with me," Derek adds, winking at Jared. "How about you, boss, maybe it's time to put these men on a diet."

Jared turns a critical eye on the men and grins. "Sounds good to me."

"Awe, come on, Derek, we were having fun with you," Jess says, tossing his paper plate in a black garbage bag tied to the side of the van.

The rest of the men echo the same thing and jump to their feet in a hurry. Five minutes later every cowhand is in the saddle, ready to go back to work.

Jared tosses me a box of syringes. "Here, Doc, you're in charge of shots. While you're at it, give 'em a good look over before turning them loose."

I look from Jared to Derek. We're standing in a perfect triangle—kind of like my relationship with the two of them. Time is suspended for a moment, like when you pause a movie to run to the kitchen for popcorn. Jared and Derek, two men so different from one another, yet in some ways the same: incredibly handsome, unattached and interested in me romantically—or at least I think Derek is still interested. I know Jared is. Both men wear lopsided grins that unnerve me, so I turn and walk toward my first patient. Branding in the 21st century is done pretty much as it was in the 1800's. The young are separated from their pregnant mothers and run, one at a time, into a cattle chute. Shots are administered, I give them a quick examination, and then one of the cowboys brands them and secures the ear tag. All this time the youngster is bellowing his or her head off. The noise is deafening—mother cows calling for their young, calves bellowing back. Even though I know this procedure guarantees the health of the herd, it always wrenches my heart.

Once the examination and shots are completed, the entire herd will be reunited until next spring when the youngsters will be separated from their mothers and sold off. This too tortures my heart but not enough to stop me from eating a good steak once in a while.

At the end of the first day I'm covered in dust. Jared decides to stay with the men. I opt to leave my horse in camp and accompany the cook back to the ranch in the van. Upon our arrival, he restocks the portable kitchen and I feed the horses in the barn. That done, I head for a well deserved bath. I enter the kitchen through the back door and notice the red light flashing on the recorder. In long, hurried strides I cross the room and depress the button. Mother's voice fills the silence.

"Hi, you two, just called to tell you the flight was absolutely wonderful. I'm in my room, standing on the balcony.

Can't tell you how excited I am to begin work with the children. If you need me, call my cell phone. Love you. Bye."

She sounds happy, I tell myself on my way upstairs.

Of course she's happy. She's doing something worthwhile with her life.

I ignore the little voice inside my head and undress while the tub fills with water. A capful of bubble bath produces a mountain of iridescent bubbles I sink beneath. Then, closing my eyes, I take a deep breath and allow my mind to wander to the day's activities. I can't deny I miss the excitement of cattle drives or the camaraderie between the cowboys. Today I was one of them, working side by side with neighboring ranchers who will expect the McChesney ranch hands to reciprocate in a few days. Life is simpler here. Neighbors help one another. Folks attend each other's weddings and funerals, and when a storm takes down a barn, someone arranges a barn raising party and half the county shows up.

The phone shatters the quiet. Leaving wet footprints on the carpet, I grab a towel and make a mad dash for Mom's bedroom while reminding myself to have the phone company out to see what they can do about the phone line in my bedroom.

"McChesney Ranch," I say, breathless.

"Just checking on you," Jared says.

The sound of his voice sends a wave of tiny fingers up my spine. My first impulse is to be sarcastic, but I curb my quick tongue, reminding myself that somewhere in the Bible it talks about the tongue being a vile, contemptible thing.

"Everything is fine. You caught me in the bathtub."

"Sorry about that." There's a pause. In the background I hear cattle calling to one another. I can almost smell the earth and the scent of night settling on the valley floor. A red campfire flickers in the blackness. Cowboys bed down near its warmth. Off in the distance a coyote wails while someone strums a guitar.

"It's okay. The water was getting cold anyway." My thoughts kick into high gear. Jared seems so close, like he's in the next room.

No static. That's unusual.

My heart stutters. "Where are you?"

"I drew first watch. You should see it, Kayla. The view I mean. I'm sitting on the hill overlooking camp. Moon's bright and the stars—well, there's plenty of them. I noticed I have cell service so the thought occurred to me to call and see if everything is all right."

Blood rushes to my face. This new, softer Jared frightens me.

"Everything is fine. I fed the horses. By the way, Mom called."

"How's she doing?"

"She's anxious to get to work and sounds happy."

A long pause follows. It isn't like Jared to have nothing to say. Eventually he clears his throat. "Sleep well. I'll see you tomorrow. You are coming out tomorrow, aren't you?"

"Of course," I reply on a yawn.

"Good. I'll let you go then. Sounds like you need to hit the sack."

Chapter 7

The phone rings, jarring me from a deep sleep. Disorientated and groggy, my eyes take their time adjusting to the pre-dawn light. I grope for my robe at the end of the bed and run down the hall to Mom's room. My reply to his, "Good morning, sleepyhead," comes on a long yawn.

"What time is it?"

Behind his voice I hear cows mooing. Instantly, my eyes fly open. "Five-thirty, Joe's waiting for you. Joe didn't want to call. He said your bedroom light wasn't on. Thought maybe you overslept?"

"The alarm didn't go off. Tell him I'll be right down."

Five minutes later I'm taking the stairs two at a time. I yank my jacket off the peg near the back door and step out into a cold breeze that signals the arrival of fall. How this happens overnight I'll never know. Skittering leaves fly across the walkway to the barn. Joe is waiting. He peers over the roof of the van and smiles. "I fed the horses for you."

Mumbling my thanks, I open the van door and slide into the passenger seat. Joe joins me. He puts the van in gear and drives around the barn, toward the back gate.

"Sorry, the alarm didn't go off," I explain.

He nods but doesn't say anything. Loyal employees don't chastise their bosses for being late, and thanks to Brandon's will, I am part owner of McChesney Ranch. Turning in my seat, I study his profile. Strong, angular jaw, graying hair, moustache, bushy eyebrows in dire need of a trim, ears and nose a bit too long for the rest of his face. Someone told me once that ears and noses continue to grow, so maybe when he was younger they fit his face.

The van bounces along the rutted fire road yet nothing seems to jostle out of place behind us. As we continue toward the waiting cowboys, the sun rises in shades of pink and orange. For a moment or two the mountain tops appear to be on fire. When the sun finally shows its face, the valley is bathed in golden light. Below us, cowboys lift their hats and wave them above their heads in anticipation of breakfast.

We are greeted with hoots and hollers and a couple complaints about us being late. For the most part the men are too hungry to tick Joe off. He doesn't tell them I'm the culprit who caused his tardiness. He goes to work quickly while the men wash up for breakfast.

Derek is no where to be seen. When I question Jared as to his whereabouts, Jared nods toward the hills. "He'll be here. Don't worry your pretty little head."

I look in the direction Jared is pointing and see a horse and rider winding their way down the steep trail toward camp. Some things never change. This throwback to times gone by sends a shiver down my spine.

"He had last watch," Jared explains and walks away.

A chill settles around me, and it has nothing to do with the brisk fall morning. With a sigh, I follow Jared to the supply boxes. His surly attitude toward my relationship with Derek gets under my skin, but I don't give him the satisfaction of a confrontation. What does bother me is that there are two sides to him: the soft, gentle Jared and the hard, callous one who is jealous and controlling.

We work side-by-side packing needles and serum. Silence separates us.

When Joe calls breakfast, I toss the last of the supplies in the box and spin on my heel. Jared remains behind. I pick up a plate and fall in line. Moments later Derek stands behind me. I know it's him by the scent of his aftershave.

Without looking, I say, "Good morning."

I hear a mumbled reply and turn around. Not thinking, I lay into him. "Look here, I tried to apologize, but you didn't give me a chance. You caught me off guard. Okay?"

Color rises into his cheeks. He looks in all directions to see if anyone is listening. Cowboys and men in general are pretty intuitive. They keep their noses out of other people's business, at least when there's an argument brewing between a guy and his girl. I'm sure that's the way they see this little tirade I'm having.

Before I get my motor running full hilt, Derek says, "Apology accepted."

Leave it up to him to stop me cold when I'm on a roll. Actually, I'm still upset with Jared for his earlier behavior, and I'm taking it out on Derek. I realize this and clamp my mouth shut before I say something stupid that I'll regret.

We're filling our plates when Derek glances sideways and gives me a lazy smile. "Feel better now?" he asks. To make sure I don't go off like a Fourth of July Firecracker, he winks.

My cheeks burn. I'm sure every ear is straining to hear our conversation. The guy in front of me turns to look over his shoulder, and I give him a warning look. He swings around and minds his own business.

Derek and I find a place to sit. We are aware of the stares but ignore them. Across the campfire from us, Jared digs into an enormous breakfast. Because of his silence, the rest of the men keep quiet. It isn't until Joe makes the rounds filling plates a second time that the men begin to talk between themselves. Thank God. Their boisterous conversation muffles Derek's invitation to dinner Friday night which I accept.

"I promise not to push. Just friends for now," he says, allaying my fears that this date will end the same as the other.

Returning his smile with a nervous chuckle, I poke another forkful of country friend potatoes into my mouth. As I chew, my eyes wander around the campsite and settle on Jared. He has his back to the rest of us, cinching the girth on his horse. A few seconds later he swings up into the saddle and yells over his shoulder.

"Let's get a move on. We've got a lot of cattle to look after."

His voice brings the men to their feet. On the way to the black trash bag they finish their breakfast and gulp the last of their coffee.

"Good vittles, Joe," rings out like a church choir.

The cowboys are saddled and ready to go in less time than it takes me to down the last dregs of coffee and collect my medical supplies. A quick look over my shoulder tells me Derek and Jared are first to arrive at the corrals. Twenty minutes later we're in full swing. I'm jabbing needles through tough hide and doing quick checkups while the frightened cattle thrash and jump inside the chute. By mid-morning I'm exhausted. Brushing a stray hair aside, I look over my shoulder to see Jared smiling at me from atop his horse.

"You need a break," he announces and dismounts.

Before I object, he removes the syringe from my hand and nods toward the cooler. "Go get yourself something cold to drink. You look a little parched."

His fingers touch mine and tiny electrical impulses run up my arm. He must feel it too because his eyes fasten on mine a moment longer than necessary. My throat tightens when he raises a hand and brushes a bit of something off my cheek. In his eyes I see my own reflection. The inside of my mouth goes dry. By the look on his face I realize that he's enjoying my reaction to his closeness. To further my embarrassment, he gives me a lazy smile and bends to whisper in my ear.

"Many women do noble things, but you surpass them all."

He's quoting from Proverbs 31.

Rather than allow him to toy with my emotions, I step aside and move toward a makeshift bathroom, nothing more than a tarp strung around a bucket. I'm greeted by a nasty odor and a horde of flies. Under these conditions I don't dawdle. As soon as I buckle my belt, I'm out of there. I go in search of shade and something cold to drink, and I run into Joe. He hands me a tall iced tea with a large wedge of lemon. I smile up into his weather-beaten face and accept his offering.

"I bet we're the only ranch in Montana that has iced tea on the range. You're a wonder, Joe. I don't know how you do it." After a long drink, I add, "Where'd you learn to cook?"

Joe doesn't talk much on a good day, unless you ask him a question. Then look out. He rests a booted foot on another stump and leans toward me. "Well, my momma thought a man should learn to cook in case he wasn't lucky enough to find a woman to do it for him." Joe gives me a lopsided grin and winks. "God bless her soul. She raised ten kids, seven of 'em boys, and without my pa 'cause he got killed in the war." Joe spins a good tale, but I'm not sure how much is true; even if fifty percent is, his mom was a saint.

By noon Jared figures we took care of five hundred head between twenty cowboys, including me. No one dallies when Joe rings the lunch bell. Weary men on horseback ride into camp. They dismount and loosen their saddle girths. Once their horses are tied to the picket lines, they gather around a communal wash basin to wait in line to rinse off the accumulation of dirt and sweat from their faces and hands. Out here, where there are no women to impress, the men wear hairy growths they won't shave off until they get home to their families.

Jared motions me to take first in line. None of the men complain. Even if they did, it wouldn't do any good. What Jared says goes. Derek slips into line behind him. I hear his voice, but I don't turn around. If I don't show partiality to either one of them in the company of the other men, Derek and Jared seem to get along just fine. It's only when you add me to the mix that it gets ugly.

The three of us take seats on make-shift benches made of lumber lying across upturned stumps. I'm in the middle, and the two men talk around me. For the most part I keep quiet. Once in a while, when asked, I give an opinion on treatment for pink eye or mastitis. Derek doesn't mention anything about our dinner date, for which I am grateful. He does, however, ask when I'm leaving for California which catches me completely off guard because I haven't thought about leaving for the past twenty-four hours; just as I haven't thought about Mom or the absence of Brandon. A pang of guilt sweeps over me. Why is it that we humans are so forgetful? The answer is simple. We are way too busy—life moves at such an incredibly fast pace, even here in Montana.

I let out a big sigh. "I haven't booked my return flight yet."

Jared doesn't let this pass. He pounces like a cat on a mouse. "If I have anything to say about it, she isn't going back." He turns and gives me one of those piercing stares that, if I was standing, would make my knees go weak. "We need a full-time vet here. Besides, it was Dad's hope that once Kayla finished her residency she would come back to Montana to practice veterinary medicine."

Put that way, how can I refuse?

But I don't agree verbally, even if I know in my heart what Jared says is true—that in the back of Brandon's mind he always hoped I'd come home. The stubborn steak in me won't bend. Agreeing to stay is like giving Jared license to run the rest of my life. At least in California I'm my own woman. Derek shifts uneasily beside me. When I turn to look at him, his eyes ask questions he doesn't dare voice out loud.

Is it true? Are you really staying?

Chapter 8

That afternoon, as we finish for the day, a cowboy rides into camp. Clouds of dust billow around the horse's hooves as he slides to a stop in front of Jared. I'm too far away to hear their conversation, but it doesn't take a genius to know something is wrong. I drop what I'm doing and run toward them. As I draw near, I hear Billy say, "We were driving them down through the draw when Charlie's horse slipped and fell. Charlie fell off and when his horse got up, he stood on Charlie's leg. It's a mess, bleeding pretty bad, might be broke."

My first thought is that Charlie has a wife and a couple kids. He can not afford to be off work. I reach for my cell phone which is fastened to my belt. No signal. Jared checks his cell phone with the same results. He thinks a minute then sends one of the men back to the ranch to arrange for an ambulance. When

I question why Joe doesn't go in the van, Jared gives me a look reserved for people who ask dumb questions.

"A horse and rider are faster. Besides, we're going to need the van to take Charlie back to the ranch." Jared turns away from me and yells for Joe. At the sound of Jared's voice, Joe tosses the dish towel aside. I don't think I've seen him move this quick in years.

Jared tells Joe there's been an accident—that Billy is in pretty bad shape.

"I'll have the men unload the van while you and Kayla pack up some medical supplies," Jared says. Another time Joe might have argued about someone messing with his cook van. Not this time. Within minutes the three of us are driving off. Billy is riding shot gun. I'm in the middle holding on tight. Joe is driving as best he can under the circumstances. Even so, the van slides sideways going down hill. For the life of me I can't figure out how he manages to keep the vehicle upright and going in the right direction. Beads of perspiration glisten on his forehead as he concentrates on the deeply rutted, steep fire roads. I breathe a sigh of relief when the van grinds to a stop.

Billy flings the door open and stumbles out while Joe and I jump out on the other side and run to the back of the vehicle. I grab the medical box. We find Charlie propped against a tree trunk, a rifle lying across his lap. A white, shiny bone protrudes through a hole in his jeans. Blood seeps from a nasty gash on his head.

I move the firearm and give Billy a hard look.

He responds with, "Charlie asked for it in case a wild animal smelled the blood."

The thought sickens me.

"It's going to be okay," I tell Charlie as I cut away the fabric to expose the compound fracture. One look and I turn to Joe. "No way can we set this out here. Hand me those splints." I stabilize Charlie's leg. When I'm done, Joe and Billy make a cradle by holding hands. Charlie takes one look at the two men and nods to me. I help him up, and he balances on one leg and leans on me. Once he's seated, he lets out a painful groan. We settle Charlie in the back of the van and tell him to hang on. Joe insists we don't need Billy, so he drops him off in camp. Start to finish, it takes two hours to get Charlie back to the ranch where an ambulance and Charlie's wife wait. Tears run down Nadine's face as she embraces her husband.

She gives Joe and me an appreciative smile and jumps into the back of the ambulance. Once the doors close, I collapse on the bumper of the van and breathe a sigh of relief. Joe echoes his own. We share a smile and congratulate each other on a job well done and get into the van. On our way back to camp, Joe gives me a long, appraising stare.

"You're a chip off the old block, you know that?"

At first I don't know what he means and then it dawns on me, he's talking about me and mom.

"How's that?" I ask.

By the look on Joe's face I'm in for a good story.

"Last year your mom rode out to see Brandon. It was just about this time of year. A cow was having a difficult delivery. The cowboys wanted to pull the calf out with a rope but your mom wouldn't hear of it. She called the practice barbaric even though it goes on all time. Rather than upset her, Brandon allowed her to play midwife, with a little help from him."

Joe's grin widens. "That calf was born right in your mom's lap. And while everyone stood around, Maggie bowed her head and gave thanks. I swear there wasn't a man around that didn't have a tear in his eye."

My eyes well up as I realize I don't know my mother at all. Long gone is the glamorous television personality. Out loud I say nothing. Inwardly, I wish I had been there to witness this touching scene.

By the time we get back to camp it's dark. Above us, God's candles shimmer in the night sky. "Something smells good," Joe says as he steps out of the van.

He ambles over to the fire pit and lifts the cover off a cast iron stew pot.

"There's some left," Derek says, pushing himself to his feet. "I'll get a couple bowls."

The rest of the men are already asleep. Jared is no where to be seen. I wonder out loud as to his whereabouts. On his way back with the bowls and eating utensils Derek says, "One of the guys saw a cougar prowling around earlier, so Jared took first watch."

Joe looks up as he ladles stew into his bowl. "Who's got second watch?"

"Billy will spell him at midnight. I'll take the early morning watch."

Derek settles beside me and watches my reaction to the stew before telling me he made it. His face creases into a boyish grin when I nod my approval.

Joe says, "Guess I'd better be careful. A young upstart like you might get ideas about wanting my job."

Derek shakes his head and chuckles. "Not a chance, my friend. I don't know how you do it day after day." He nods to the row of sleeping bags. "They're a tough bunch to please."

Joe mops the last of his stew up with a slice of bread and excuses himself. Ten minutes later the night is quiet, except for the snap of burning logs and the occasional coyote. I lean back and stare at the orange embers.

"Penny for your thoughts," Derek says, not very original but it gets me started.

I let out a sigh and ask if he really wants to know. He nods. I tell him about the emotional roller coaster I've been on for twelve years. I confess I still think about Hunter a lot. I also tell him how confused I was the day he kissed me at the Cow Palace after my big win. I don't hold anything back. When I come up for air, Derek is smiling.

"I'm sorry I added to your problems. But you were too young, and I was on the rebound. Besides, you were Jared's girl. He made that abundantly clear."

His being candid gives me the boldness to say, "I wasn't Jared's girl. And furthermore, you broke my heart."

In a low voice he asks, "And what about now. Is your heart still broken or have you forgiven me?"

His eyes twinkle in the firelight. I find myself wishing he would kiss me but then I remember telling him not to do that again. Being this close to him stirs something within me. I raise my chin and look into his eyes. I sense he feels the same thing I do. He runs the tip of his tongue over his upper lip and says, "Dog gone it, Kayla, if you expect me to just sit here and pretend I don't have feelings for you, think again."

He reaches out and pulls me into his arms. Somewhere behind us one of the cowboys yells, "For pity sake, kiss her and get it over with so the rest of us can get a decent night's sleep."

My face feels warm from embarrassment. Derek, however, doesn't seem to care one way or the other that our entire conversation is overheard. He lowers his lips to mine and kisses me, not once but twice. When our lips part he whispers, "That wasn't so bad, was it?"

The Friday of our date, Derek calls to tell me there's a problem with one of the men he is counseling. Even though I'm disappointed, I tell him not to worry.

"We'll do it another time."

He thanks me for understanding and hangs up.

About that time Jared comes in. He gives me a long look and raises an amused eyebrow. "All this for me?" he asks. His arrogance sets my teeth on edge. I bite back a smart reply and tell him what happened and why I'm standing in the kitchen, dressed to the nines. I see that he isn't the least bit unhappy for me. On his way through the kitchen, he says, "Well, I can't let a nice dress like that go unnoticed. Give me a few minutes and we'll have dinner."

Before I can object, he's gone.

Ten minutes later he comes downstairs wearing a light brown sports jacket with suede patches on the elbows, dark brown slacks and loafers. Even if I don't like him, I have to admit he cleans up nicely. He catches me staring and gives me a lazy grin on his way to get my coat from the hall closet.

"Ready?" he asks, holding it open for me to slide my arms into.

We step out into a brisk fall evening. Jared takes my elbow and ushers me to the Suburban, which is parked at the end of the walkway. Breath floats out in front of him as he asks, "What do you feel like? Italian, Mediterranean, McDonalds?" He opens the door and waits until I'm seated. "You pick."

The look on his face says we're not leaving until I choose. "How about Perugia Old World Cooking?"

"That's that place on West Broadway Street, right?"

I nod, and he closes the door.

With a sigh of resignation I'm prepared to have an awful evening. To my surprise, Jared is both charming and talkative. He never mentions Derek. Once we're seated in the restaurant, he orders coffee. And later, with all the wonderful items on the menu, we both order a steak. Our conversation is light, nothing earthshaking. While we eat, Jared recalls our first meeting with vivid clarity. I wonder where he's going with this when he says,

"Seems so long ago, doesn't it?" His eyes find mine and stay there. "I really blew it back then. I mean…well you know what I mean—putting pressure on you when you were just a kid."

I smile and say, "But it's all right to pressure me now?"

He shakes his head. "No, it's not all right. I guess it shows how insecure I am when it comes to us."

I almost say 'there is no us', but something stops me. Until now Jared and I have avoided talking about our past, but since he brings it up, I put in my two cents. "Yes, you were pushy. Actually, you still are. You don't give me a chance to like you. What I mean is, just about the time I decide you have some redeeming qualities you do or say something hateful. Why is that? And why do you have to control everything?"

Jared chuckles and holds up his hand as if to ward off my attack. "Truce," he calls out just as the waiter arrives at our table.

We decline dessert and Jared asks for the check.

On the drive home we agree to treat each other with mutual respect. He leaves me at the bottom of the stairs and avoids an awkward moment by telling me that he wants to watch the weather report.

I'm halfway up when I turn. The way he's watching me brings color to my cheeks. "I had a nice time," I say and continue up the staircase.

"I did too," he replies.

Snow covers the ground, and it's only the first week in October. Mom calls every Tuesday evening, regular as clockwork. It's understood that I will not return to California even though I haven't said so yet. Derek and I agree to take it one day at a time. Mom is elated. She's always cared deeply for Derek. On the other hand, Jared isn't making this easy. He finds extra work for Derek on days we are planning dinner and a movie. Derek never complains. He doesn't want to make life miserable for me, but I can tell he's had enough.

Today the phone rings early. It's not Tuesday, so I wonder who might be calling at six in the morning. Derek tells me one of the men he's been counseling committed suicide.

"None of us saw it coming," he says. I can tell he's near tears. "Makes me feel like I failed him," he adds, sniffing.

"Don't do that to yourself."

There's so much pain in his voice.

"It's kind of hard not to. I was the last one to see him."

A long silence follows and then Derek says, "Tell Jared I won't be there today. I want to be with the man's family. They're going to need all the support they can get."

"Of course, and let me know if I can help. You will, won't you?"

He says he'll call if there's anything I can do and then hangs up. That's when Jared walks into the kitchen.

"Who was that?" he asks on his way to the coffee pot.

I draw a breath. "Derek. One of the men he's been working with killed himself last night. Derek won't be here today. He wants to be with the man's family."

Jared pours milk into his cup, adds coffee and turns to face me. He takes a sip and then moves toward the table where I've set out a plate of bacon and eggs, toast and juice. Once he's seated, he says, "Derek's heart isn't in ranching any more. He'll make a mighty fine preacher though."

Now that Jared mentions it, I can see Derek standing in the pulpit preaching the gospel or ministering to a dying man or woman. And he's good with kids of all ages. Maybe he'll be a youth pastor. I chuckle at the thought and then my face sobers.

What I can't see is me being a preacher's wife.

J. B. Williams

Chapter 9

I didn't know Bruce Howard. Even so, I accept Derek's invitation to the memorial service. When we arrive at the church, an impeccably groomed, elderly woman greets us. Her hair is snow white, falling in gentle curls to her shoulders. Sunglasses hide her eyes. A gentleman in his late forties, stylishly dressed, wearing a tweed topcoat over a dark suit stands beside her.

As we walk toward them, Derek bends toward me and whispers, "Kevin is Bruce's older brother."

Derek introduces me as Maggie McChesney's daughter. The fact I'm Maggie's daughter is of little consequence to Kevin. Not so with his mother. Mrs. Howard's face brightens. She grasps my hand and squeezes it like we're old friends.

"Your mother is a wonderful woman, but I don't have to tell you that. Do I?"

I shake my head and smile. I learn that Mrs. Howard worked with my mother on several church committees including women's ministry.

"Your mother does so much for those in need. She's generous to a fault. If she hears about someone down on their luck, she brings them groceries and assists them in finding employment." Mrs. Howard waves a gloved hand to the inside of the church. "And thanks to your mother, we have stained glass windows. They add so much to our worship service."

She thanks me for coming and turns her attention to Derek who has been standing beside me all this time. As if she remembers why we are here, her lip trembles. Derek gathers her in his arms, and I find myself strangely uncomfortable in their presence. The man I think I know, I don't know at all.

Jared's voice echoes in my head.

Derek's heart isn't in ranching any more. He'd make a mighty fine preacher, though.

Standing to one side, I observe Mrs. Howard and Kevin as they greet Bruce's friends. All the right words are said. They accept every heartfelt condolence with dignity. But it's Derek I'm worried about. He feels he let Bruce down.

When the last guest is seated, Derek reaches for my hand and smiles down at me. He gives my fingers a little squeeze as we follow Mrs. Howard and Kevin to the front of the church. From my place in first pew, I stare at the life-sized picture of Bruce Howard displayed on an easel near the altar. The organist plays Amazing Grace. On the final cord, Derek rises and walks to the pulpit. In his absence, Mrs. Howard scoots over to sit next to me. For the next fifteen minutes I am caught up in the life of Bruce Howard as told by Derek. He concludes his eulogy by assuring each of us that God is just and faithful to forgive our sins—all we have to do is ask.

How long has it been since you asked for forgiveness?

I look sideways to see if Mrs. Howard hears the voice too, but her eyes are riveted on Derek. A lone tear slides down her wrinkled cheek.

"I don't know the condition of Bruce's heart the day he met his Savior," Derek says as he looks out over the congregation. "But I do know Bruce loved the Lord very much."

I hear "Amen" from the rear of the church and then another.

Derek's eyes peruse the gathering before settling on Mrs. Howard and Kevin. They smile at one another, and then

Derek motions everyone to stand. "Please join me in the Lord's Prayer."

After the 'amen' Derek invites those who want to speak to step up to the microphone. An uncomfortable silence follows. Derek waits. He smiles encouragement at Kevin who finally comes forward. Teary-eyed, Kevin reminisces about a particularly fond memory of his brother when they were little boys. I reach for a tissue in my purse and dab at my eyes. My heart is still raw from losing Brandon. I guess that's why I identify with the speaker's loss. Or maybe it's because I never really let loose and cried. In any case, tears spill down my cheeks unchecked, and by the time the last speaker leaves the podium, I feel as if I know Bruce Howard the son, brother and friend and not just the despondent man who took his own life.

After the service, six men carry the mahogany casket from the church. This is the first time I see Mrs. Howard cry. The inside of the church is silent, except for the sound of her convulsive sobs. Because it is customary for the congregation to wait for the family to leave, they remain seated while Derek consoles her. When she stops crying, he takes her arm and leads her toward the back of the church. Kevin and I follow a few feet behind, and the rest of the congregation walks behind us. It isn't until we reach the last row that I notice Jared standing near the doorway. He greets Mrs. Howard with open arms. They speak for a few moments and then Jared greets Derek. I don't know why I'm surprised to see him here. The McChesney family knows everyone within a hundred miles.

A brisk wind sweeps down from the north and sends a cold chill down my spine. Jared offers me his arm, and we follow Derek, Kevin and Mrs. Howard as they walk behind the casket. In the middle of the tiny cemetery is a mound of dirt covered by artificial turf. By the time we arrive at the gravesite, the casket is waiting to be lowered into the open grave. The wind wails through the naked tree branches overhead as Derek helps Mrs. Howard to her seat. Her face is veiled in grief as she prepares to say goodbye. When everyone is in place, Derek stands to read the 23rd Psalm. Following the reading, he asks that we join him in singing Bruce's favorite song. I can't help but smile when Derek begins to sing *What a Friend We Have In Jesus.*

Later, in the small gathering room adjacent to the church, I have a chance to speak with Jared alone since Derek is with Mrs. Howard and her son. We go through the buffet line together and take our plates to a table in the corner of the room. Once we're seated, I turn to him.

"You knew, didn't you?"

"Knew what?" he asks.

"That Derek was officiating at the service."

Jared weighs his words, something he doesn't do often. "Yes, Derek told me when he called to ask for a few days off."

Between bites I give him a curious smile he pretends not to see. I wait a few seconds. "That was very nice of you." He shrugs off my compliment and dives into his food. A few minutes pass. In that time Jared doesn't look at me. He is completely devoted to the slice of ham that takes up half his plate.

I break the silence between us. "I know you're short handed with Charlie being laid up and Derek taking a few days off. If there's anything I can do, let me know."

He looks up from his plate. "Thanks, I appreciate that."

His politeness is driving me crazy. I'm about to ask him about the stained glass windows when a hand comes to rest on my shoulder. I close my mouth and look up into a pair of smiling eyes.

"Nathan! My goodness, how are you doing?"

I set my fork aside and stand. Nathan, a high school friend I haven't seen in ten years, towers over me. The first thing to cross my mind is that he isn't the clumsy hulk I remember. He's dressed in a tailored suit and slacks. His blond hair has receded a bit, but his smile hasn't changed.

"I thought that was you," he says. He gives Jared a cursory glance and nods. "How's it going, Jared?"

"Can't complain," Jared replies and stands. "If you two will excuse me, I see the ladies are putting out dessert."

With Jared out of the way, Nathan and I catch up on old times. He coaches the football team at the high school we attended. He's never been married, which surprises me. Then he tells me his mother died of breast cancer a few years ago. I murmur how sorry I am to hear that and fill him in on the last twelve years of my life. By the time Jared returns, we've made a date to have lunch on Saturday.

Nathan says goodbye and walks across the floor to a table where several people are gathered. I watch him pull up a chair and sit. Moments later he's engrossed in conversation.

I turn to Jared, who at the moment is putting a very large helping of pineapple upside down cake into his mouth.

"Nathan hasn't changed a bit, has he?" I say.

"Nope, he's the same old Nathan. The man's got a one track mind. Football."

I don't tell him they have something in common then. As I see it, Jared thinks only of cattle. I don't get the chance because Derek sits beside me. He apologizes for getting sidetracked, and I assure him I understand that Mrs. Howard needs him. When I add, "more than I do," his face falls. I quickly correct my mistake. "You know what I mean. She just lost her son."

Jared leans back in his chair, arms across his chest and smiles at us.

Rather than give him the pleasure of blushing, I turn to Derek and compliment him on a job well done. I guess this little bit of intimacy annoys Jared because he clears his throat and pushes his chair back with a noisy scrape. Standing, he excuses himself to say his goodbyes to the bereaved family. Now that Jared is gone, Derek turns to me. "I hope you understand if I drive Mrs. Howard and her son home. She doesn't drive. Apparently they called a cab to bring them to church. I wish I'd known …"

Derek's voice trails off. He looks across the room to where Jared is bent over Mrs. Howard. "Would you mind riding home with Jared?" he asks.

Yes, I mind. I came with you. I want to leave with you.

I smile and tell him I don't mind. "No trouble at all," I add, gathering my coat and purse. I push the chair back and stand. "I'd better hurry. It's looks like he's getting ready to leave."

I meet Jared on his way to retrieve his coat from the coat closet near the entrance. When I ask him for a lift home, he gives me a strange look. I don't want him to think I'm the sort of woman who comes with one man and leaves with another, so I explain in a quiet voice that Derek is driving Kevin and Mrs. Howard home and that he intends to stay with them in their time of need.

"I want to say goodbye to Mrs. Howard and Kevin before we leave," I tell him.

He follows me across the room but is stopped by one of the neighboring ranchers along the way. I count this a blessing because Mrs. Howard solicits my promise to drop by for tea one afternoon and insists I bring Derek with me.

On the way home Jared is unusually quiet. When I ask if there is something bothering him, he turns and says, "Death. It's so final." He concentrates on the road for several minutes before turning to me again. "Do you really believe in life after death?"

His question takes me by surprise. While I'm formulating my answer, he says, "There's this voice in my head that tells me it's all a hoax and that God doesn't exist."

I can't help but smile. "That happens to me all the time," I assure him.

His eyes brighten with hope. "It does?"

I nod. "When it does, I do what my mom told me to do when I was a little kid, I pray the Devil away."

This simplistic approach causes Jared to chuckle. It also lightens his mood considerably.

It's after six when we walk through the front door, into a cold house. Jared turns up the thermostat and helps me off with my coat. He hangs his and mine in the closet and heads for the kitchen. I trail after him. While he makes hot chocolate, I thumb through the mail left on the table by one of the hired hands. There's a letter addressed to me from Mom, which I tuck into my pocket to read in private.

"Nothing but advertisements," I mumble.

He hands me my cup of cocoa. We sit down at the table and stare at each other over the rims of our cups. The kitchen is quiet, except for the tick of the clock. Finally he says, "So, did Nathan ask you out?"

His question comes from left field. I think about telling him it's none of his business. Instead I say, "Yes, as a matter of fact he did. It will be fun to catch up on old times."

He studies me for a long moment before asking, "How does it feel to have three men vying for your affection?"

It's not what he says, but how he says it that causes me to react. In a less than friendly tone I remind him I'm not in the market for a husband.

"I have a career I have put on hold until mother returns. Remember?"

"So, you're leaving as soon as Maggie gets back?"

I don't tell him I had thoughts of staying on. I see now that would be impossible. We'd be at each other's throats the first time he intruded into my private life.

And Mom would be right in the middle of it.

J. B. Williams

Chapter 10

I feel certain that Jared's eyes are on my back as I leave the kitchen. I don't care. Exhaustion permeates my body as I climb the stairs with one thought in mind: What possessed me to think I could stay here? I do a quick wash, brush my teeth and apply moisturizer to my face. As I leave the bathroom, I hear Jared's footsteps. I hurry down the hall, into my bedroom. Quietly, so he doesn't hear, I close the door and listen for him. He goes into the bathroom. Moment's later I hear the click of his bedroom door.

Once the house is quiet, I change into pajamas and read Mom's letter. It starts out by assuring me she's enjoying every minute with the children.

I can't tell you how gratifying it is to bring Jesus to these children. The people who run the orphanage are doing the best they can. Even so, the children are starved for love and attention. They don't ask for much, just a warm bed and enough food to eat. The conditions here are worse than I imagined. If Brandon were here, he'd tear this place down. So, that's what I'm going to do. I've contacted the bank in Missoula and instructed them to wire enough money to build a girl's dormitory. And the kind people at the consulate have worked a miracle. I will be allowed to stay an additional two months so I can see the completed project. Isn't that exciting? I couldn't do this if you weren't there, you know. Jared can be a bit controlling at times, but he has a good heart. He's not much good at keeping house, laundry or paying the bills so in my absenc, please write checks using the power of attorney I left.

I hope my staying on a while longer won't inconvenience you. You did tell me you asked for a leave of absence to help take care of things. If for some reason you decide to return to California, please forward all mail to Sarah and leave the checkbook with her.

Aunt Sarah. I haven't seen her since the funeral. Rebecca, her daughter is twelve. To help with finances, Aunt Sarah returned to her teaching job. Uncle Frank works days as an auto mechanic and runs their ranch evenings and weekends. Feeling guilty, I make a mental note to call them later and continue to read.

There's one person in particular I hope to help. She is blind and has been since an automobile accident several years ago. I met her at the orphanage. She is a volunteer here. Isn't that amazing? Laura is your age. The doctors say an operation might restore her sight. Her parents are deceased and she has no brothers or sisters. I've asked her to return to America with me, but Laura is giving me a bit of trouble right now. She doesn't want to leave the kids, but I will wear her down.

Love,

Mom

Between the lines I read the excitement in Mom's voice. Part of me is happy for her; the other part doesn't want to share her, especially not with a stranger.

Is Laura the reason she doesn't care if I go back to California?

Mom's words echo in my head.

If you decide to go back to California, take the check book over to your Aunt Sarah.

I put the letter in the desk drawer and turn to face the mirror over the dresser. Leaving isn't an option. Not when Mom is bringing home a total stranger to live in her home. The clock on the nightstand reads ten. Quickly, before I change my mind,

I dig in my purse and find my cell phone. Roger picks up on the first ring.

"Hello."

"Roger, something has come up. I hate to do this to you on such short notice, but I'm calling to turn in my resignation."

He groans like someone kicked him in the gut.

"I knew this would happen. I told Jessie you wouldn't come back."

"I'm sorry. I really am. Mom's in Romania. She's volunteering at an orphanage."

"So, what's that got to do with you. When you left you said it would only be for a few weeks. It's been a couple months for cripes sakes. Everyone's been pulling double duty because of you."

No way am I going to tell him I'm staying because I'm a jealous daughter who is worried her Mom is bringing a gold digger back with her. Even thinking it makes me sound unchristian-like.

"Don't tell me you're going to marry that control freak and have a bunch of snot-nosed kids?"

Roger doesn't talk to kids, he growls at them. He's forty-eight and never been married. I recall the day he told me what he thought about marriage.

"Since I don't intend to procreate, there's no reason to get married," he said in a matter of fact tone.

"Of course not," I reply. "I'm staying because mother needs me."

"Yeah, sure, so what are you going to do with your condo?"

This is where I tiptoe lightly. "Well, I was hoping you and Jessie might oversee renting it out for me. You can have anything above expenses for managing the property." Before he raises a fit, I add, "Maybe Jessie would like to earn some extra money packing up my stuff. I'll rent it furnished. All she has to do is pack my bedroom and office."

Roger lets out a long, frustrated sigh. "Let me think on it tonight. I'll talk with Jessie in the morning and call you. Bye."

The phone clicks in my ear.

At least he doesn't tell me to fly back and do it myself. I crawl between the sheets and turn out the light. Closing my eyes, I try to put Mom's letter out of my head, but the forced air heat comes on and keeps me awake. This is as good a time as any to confess my jealousy to God. I tell him how sorry I am to disappoint him yet another time. I complain about Jared and ask Him to change Jared so he's easier to like. I pray for Mom. I ask Him to protect her and give her wisdom so she will see that her decision to bring Laura here is a mistake. On and on I go and then it occurs to me, I am selfish. Instead of thanking God for all the good things in my life, I ask Him to change people so they conform to my liking. Unable to sleep, I sit up and turn on the light. I search in the nightstand drawer for the Bible I tucked there when I unpacked. At home my Bible lies on the coffee table gathering dust like an ornament—an outward sign to anyone who visits me that I am a Christian. Truth be known, I don't open it often enough. So, when I turn to James and begin to read, tears fill my eyes. The book of James tells me how to live to please God. It's a mirror that reveals the real me, a self-centered woman who is easily provoked and doesn't look for the good in people. I find it easy to love the loveable but hard to love the unlovable. Jared immediately comes to mind.

Yet to love is a commandment from God.

My eyes blur as I read.

Do not merely listen to the word, and so deceive yourselves. Do what it says. Anyone who listens to the word but does not do what it says is like a man who looks at his face in a mirror and, after looking at himself, goes away and immediately forgets what he looks like.

The book of James is short, five chapters. I read and reread it until the downstairs clock strikes one. Before I close my eyes, I pray to be more like God. "Help me see the good in

Jared, Lord. And when Laura arrives, help me welcome her as you would welcome her."

The following morning I awake refreshed. I call Aunt Sarah before she leaves for work and ask if it will be all right if I drop by later in the day. She is delighted to hear my voice.

"Why haven't you called earlier?" she asks.

I catch her up to date on the happenings of the past few weeks. When I get to Mom's letter, she acts as if she knows. But why shouldn't she know? She's my mother's sister. They share everything. I remind myself that if I had a sister I would do the same.

"You don't sound very enthused," Aunt Sarah says.

I never could hide my feelings from her. "Can we talk about this later?" I ask with an eye on my watch. "It's half past seven. You'll be late for work." Before I hang up I tell her not to cook. "I'll bring pizza for dinner."

Noise downstairs in the kitchen spurs me to dress in a hurry. I find Jared whipping up batter for waffles. Sausage sizzles in a frying pan, coffee perks on the countertop. He gives me a lopsided grin. "Hope you're hungry," he says, nodding to the frying pan.

On my way to pour a cup of coffee, I peek in the frying pan and raise my eyebrows in surprise. "Why so many sausages, are you expecting guests?"

His cheeks turn pink. "I forgot to take them out of the freezer. I figured if I cooked them all now, we could reheat them tomorrow."

"Good thinking."

Once we are seated, I hand him Mom's letter. Part of me hopes he will agree with me about Laura.

Jared's eyes run down the page. Unlike me, he grins as he reads. My guess is he knows I'm watching him. He looks up from the letter. "Just like Maggie to extend her stay," he says, locking eyes with mine.

"Read on," I tell him.

When he finishes the letter, he hands it to me and waits for my reaction to the news.

"So, how do you feel about this?" I ask.

He shrugs and stuffs a forkful of sausage in his mouth. His nonchalance ticks me off. He should have an opinion. I do.

"Aren't you the least bit concerned that my mother, your stepmother, is bringing a stranger to our home, a blind one at tha! I get the impression she's thinking of covering the expenses for her eye surgery."

Jared looks at me like I'm from another planet. He sets his fork down, wipes his mouth on a napkin and rests his elbows on the table. Lacing his fingers together, he stares at me for a long uncomfortable time as his eyes search mine.

"Do you really want to know what I think?"

"Yes, I want to know what you think or I wouldn't ask."

After a long pause, he says, "If you're honest with yourself, you don't want to share Maggie with another woman. It has nothing to do with money or that Laura is blind."

Jared finishes off the last of his eggs and takes his plate to the sink. The tension between us thickens as he rinses his dishes and utensils and puts them in the dishwasher. I am ready to explode when a verse from the book of James ops into my head.

The tongue also is a fire, a world of evil among the parts of the body. It corrupts the whole person...

Recalling my promise of the night before, I remain silent. Jared finishes up the dishes and turns around. We look at one another a long time and then I get up and carry my dishes to the sink. He moves over to allow me room to rinse the dishes off before putting them in the dishwasher.

"You're not going to take my head off?" he asks.

I stare at the running water splashing over the dish and shake my head. "No, I'm not going to bite your head off. You have a right to your opinions," I reply, turning to face him.

The surprise on his face makes me laugh. It also eases the tension between us. He pours another cup of coffee and leans against the counter. I pour another cup and lean against the stove. We discuss Mom's decision to stay on in Romania a while longer and ease our way into her decision to bring Laura home. Jared's generosity amazes me.

"We have more than enough. If Maggie wants to help Laura regain her sight, then I think the two of us should support her decision." A wistful smile transforms his face. "Besides, Dad would be proud of her. Don't you think?"

Both of us are a bit unsure of this new, friendlier relationship. I nod my agreement to which Jared announces he has a long day ahead of him. When our eyes meet, I glance away. Silly I know, but I can't look him directly in the eyes. Especially in a situation like this when he shows me the nicer, softer side of him.

Jared tosses the rest of his coffee down the drain and pulls a jacket off the peg near the back door. Before he leaves, I tell him I won't be home for dinner. I qualify that with, "I'm spending the evening with Uncle Frank and Aunt Sarah. I haven't seen them since the funeral."

He nods and goes out the back door. I stand there for a moment. If I was truly trying to be nicer to him, I'd invite him to have pizza with us. I start toward the door and change my mind. After all, I'm entitled to talk with Aunt Sarah and Uncle Frank alone.

I take a quick shower, dress in jeans and boots and go down to the barn. Jared's truck isn't in the driveway. The barn is quiet except for the munching of oats. I stop at Lady's stall and peek in. To my horror, she's laying flat in the hay. She hasn't touched her oats. Sweat glistens on her neck and shoulders. Quietly, so I don't upset her, I slide the door open and walk in. Lady lifts her head and grunts. I don't have a stethoscope with me, so I can't listen to her gut. I do a hydration test by pinching her skin together with my fingers. When I let go, it takes a long time to smooth out. I check her gums. They are turning gray, another indication she is dehydrated. This happens a lot with horses. When the weather changes, they don't drink enough water and the hay becomes impacted in their intestines. They get a belly ache and lay down to roll. This is when the intestines twist, causing the horse terrible pain. The only recourse is to take the horse into surgery and cut the damaged length of intestine out and reconnect the good intestine.

I slide the stall door open and run to the office. The door is locked. For a moment my heart stops, then I remember the cell phone in my pocket and take it out. Jared answers, and I give him the details as quickly as I can.

"I'll call the vet. Stay with her," he says and hangs up.

I run back to Lady's stall and put a halter on her head. Even though I don't want to, I use the end of the lead rope to smack her on the hindquarters to urge her to get up.

"You have to get up, girl. If you don't you're going to die."

Lady seems to understand the severity of her predicament. She rises up on her sternum and from there she sits up on her hindquarters. She rocks twice and stands on wobbly legs.

"Come on, girl, we're going to the arena to walk your tummy ache off," I tell her.

She doesn't move, and I swat her hind end with the lead rope. On the way to the arena she tries to lie down. I swat her again to urge her on. She's in terrible pain, but I know if she rolls, she's liable to twist a gut and that will likely be the end of her.

We're walking the perimeter of the arena when Jared pulls up. I hear his truck tires stop on the rocks. Moment's later he's in the arena with me. He walks behind Lady, and every time she tries to go down, he hits her on the hindquarters with his old Stetson.

"Where the heck is he?" he asks, referring to the vet.

"I wish I had my vet truck," I moan.

Lady is beginning to tire. She wants to go down. Nothing we do stops her. She collapses in the sand just as the vet shows up. Neither of us recognizes him. He introduces himself as Thad Stevens, the new guy at the clinic and then presses the stethoscope to Lady's side. He listens. The look on his face tells it all. Lady is in trouble.

"How long has she been like this?" he asks.

Jared turns to me.

"I don't know. I found her down an hour ago," I say.

I watch while Thad pulls on a latex glove. He douses the glove with lubricant and glances sideways at me. "You're a vet, right?"

"Yes."

"That's what I thought. Large animals, right?"

I nod.

"Then I don't have to tell you what I'm looking for. If she has a twist, we'll need to transport her to the veterinary hospital right away. How old is she?"

Jared answers. "Eighteen."

Thad eases his arm inside Lady's rectum. She groans. He doesn't get far. His face turns ashen. He withdraws his arm and shakes his head. No one says a word. He gives Lady a small sedative while Jared hooks up the trailer. Fifteen minutes later we pull into the veterinary hospital. Two technicians meet us. Things happen quickly. They x-rays they take of Lady's intestines confirm Thad's diagnosis. Her gut is twisted. Jared signs a consent form and she's prepared for surgery. When Thad arrives, he asks if I want to scrub and assist in surgery. I shake my head and watch him disappears into the clinic.

"Why didn't you scrub?" Jared asks.

"I don't know. I just think it would be best for Lady if I stay out here and pray instead." I'm riddled with guilt. Since coming home I haven't spent much time with her. It is uncanny how Jared reads my mind. He tells me everything will be okay and wraps an arm around my shoulder. Together we walk to the waiting room.

I slump in a chair. He paces. Finally he says, "Let's go get a cup of coffee. I'll leave my cell number with them."

We stop at the reception desk and leave his telephone number.

On the way to the coffee shop, Jared turns to me. Lines furrow his brow. "She's in a lot of trouble, isn't she?"

"Yes."

He hesitates before asking, "What are her chances?"

I find it difficult to speak. More than once I have had to break the news to an owner that their horse died on the operating table. "Age is against her."

"What will they do?"

"Sometimes they have to pull the intestines out and lay them on a table. Depending upon how bad the twist is and how long it's been there; he will either untwist the gut or cut the damaged part out and reconnect. It's a gamble either way. I'd rather remove stones. All you have to do is find the thing and take it out; a much smaller incision in most cases. If Lady's gut has shut down, there's a chance we could lose her."

J. B. Williams

Chapter 11

If the operation went as planned, Lady should be in recovery. I don't tell Jared I have doubts. Instead, I stare at my half-eaten bowl of chili so he can't read the worry in my eyes. The waitress offers me a coffee refill. I manage a smile and decline. Jared nods, and she pours his seventh or eighth cup. Out of the corner of my eye, I watch Jared pour cream into the mud-colored liquid. He stirs the mixture absently and then brings the cup to his lips. Moments later he swivels his stool to face me.

"We should hear something soon, shouldn't we?"

The words barely leave his mouth when his cell phone rings. He gives me a nervous smile and flips the phone open.

"This is Jared McChesney." I mistake his sigh of relief for good news, and then I realize my optimism is a bit premature. I watch him fight for composure and think the worst as tears well up and roll down my cheeks. Through blurry eyes I see Jared nod as if the person on the other end is right in front of him. "We'll be right there," Jared says and snaps the phone shut.

He stares at me for a long time, unable to speak.

"She didn't make … it, did she?"

He blows out a breath of air and gives me an uncertain smile. "Thad doesn't want us to get our hopes up yet. He says the next few hours will be critical." Jared smiles with confidence. "But she came through it, so there's hope, right?"

Relief washes over me. I'm laughing and crying when I leap into his arms. He's laughing too. The diners stare at us, but we don't care. We hold each other for a long moment before Jared releases me with am embarrassed smile. He tosses money on the counter, and we dash out of the coffee shop as if we just robbed the place.

"Thank you, Lord," I say out loud.

"Amen to that," Jared agrees.

We leave quickly and arrive at the clinic in record time. Jared jumps out and beats me to the door. Inside we are greeted by a nurse who informs us she assisted Thad in surgery.

"Can we see her?" Jared asks in eager anticipation.

The nurse smiles and holds her hand up to slow him down. "Lady isn't out from under the anesthetic yet."

Jared turns to me for an explanation. "Shouldn't she be awake by now?"

"It takes time. Every case is different," I tell him.

The nurse says Thad wants me to suit up and join him in the recovery unit. I glance at Jared, unsure of how he will take this solo invitation.

He nods. "One of us should be with her."

"Are you sure?"

"Yes."

I'm led into a room where I scrub my hands and arms up to my elbows. Then I'm helped into green scrubs, given a cap to cover my hair and a mask to cover my mouth and nose. Another woman pulls booties over my tennis shoes and helps me into latex gloves. The veterinary assistant opens the door to a padded, cell-like room and steps aside. All the years working as a vet don't help when it comes to Lady. My heart stops at the sight of her standing with her feet splayed apart, head bobbing up and down, a plastic bag hanging from an overhead arm. Attached to the bag is long tube which is attached to an intravenous needle that is inserted into a vein in Lady's neck.

"Fluids," Thad whispers, nodding to the bag.

A horse coming out from under anesthesia is sometimes startled by unfamiliar noises, so we speak in quiet tones.

"We took out a foot of gut. It's a wait and see situation. You know the drill. If the bowels begin to move, we're one step closer to saving her."

Out of habit I pinch Lady's skin. It's very loose. "Not good."

Thad smiles behind his mask. "Give it time." He hesitates and moves toward the door. "Since you're here, I think I'll go see what's next on the agenda." He points to a wall phone near the door. "If things go wrong, buzz me."

I nod and watch the door close behind him.

Twenty minutes later Lady lifts her head and recognizes me. The rope attached to her halter is tethered to the wall. She can't go anywhere, so I feel comfortable using the phone. On the wall next to the phone is a list of numbers. I run my finger down the column until I find the reception desk. A pleasant voice says, "Is everything all right in there?"

"Yes, is Jared still sitting in the waiting area?"

"Yes, he is."

"Could you tell him Lady is coming around? Another thing, could you please ask him to call Sarah and tell her I won't be stopping by this evening?"

With one eye on Lady, I listen to the receptionist converse with Jared. She returns to the phone and tells me he's calling as we speak. "Is there anything else I can do for you?" she asks in a pleasant voice.

"Yes, please inform Dr. Stevens Lady is coming around."

Moments later Thad comes in. He checks Lady's heart and gums before pressing a stethoscope against her side. He's listening for gut noise.

"Yes," he says, grinning at me.

He has kind eyes. On the tail end of that thought I reprimand myself for noticing at a time like this. I wait for him to do all the things I would do under the circumstances and when he finishes his exam, he hands me the stethoscope.

I hesitate. "Go on, have a listen. I think you'll be pleasantly surprised."

The tiny lines that frame his eyes are a dead giveaway to a smile beneath his surgical mask.

I press the stethoscope against Lady's side and hear a small gurgle. I look up at Thad and nod.

"Unless infection sets in, Lady is on the long road to recovery," he says.

"Thank you so much. You did a fine job."

His eyes linger on mine a moment longer than necessary when I hand him the stethoscope. I don't know why, but I find myself not handling this very well. To divert his attention from me, I nod toward the door. "Would it be okay if Jared comes in for a minute?"

"Of course, but just for a few minutes. I suggest the two of you go home. There's an excellent night nurse here to monitor Lady's progress. I'll leave word that if anything changes she's to call me first, then you."

Thad picks up the phone and calls the front desk. "Help Mr. McChesney into a gown and mask, and make sure he's wearing booties and gloves."

When Jared enters the room, Thad reiterates what he's already told me. "Infection is our enemy right now. She's on antibiotics. Let's keep our fingers crossed."

Jared nods and moves toward Lady. He talks to her in quiet tones. I can see he is visibly shaken. Thad notices too.

"Why don't the two of you go home, you can come back tomorrow and sit with her," he says, moving us toward the door.

In the changing room, Jared and I take off our masks and booties which we toss in the trash receptacle. We take off our gowns and throw them in the laundry basket. Thad meets us in the reception area. He shakes hands with Jared and pats me on the shoulder.

"See you in the morning," he says and escorts us out the door.

I swing around in my seat when Jared drives past the iron gates of McChesney ranch. "Where are we going? I ask even though I know our destination. He glances at me. In the lights of the oncoming car I see him smile.

"Sarah said to come over even if it's late. I promised her we would. She's holding dinner for us."

Jared gets no argument from me or my stomach, which growls loud enough for him to hear. He chuckles and steps on the gas. The vehicle responds.

"We'd better hurry before you starve to death," he says.

The levity between us feels good. It's been a long time since we've been this comfortable together. In times like this I can almost envision us living in the same house without butting heads.

Aunt Sarah greets us at the door. Uncle Frank is right behind her. Once we are inside, the two of them fire questions at us. We're bombarded a second time when Rebecca comes downstairs. I can't believe how big she is. Looking at her, I realize she resembles mom more than Aunt Sarah. Rebecca is tall and slim, with dark hair and dancing eyes. She has freckles and talks non-stop.

"If she doesn't get an infection, Thad thinks she should be okay," I tell Rebecca who scrunches up her face at the thought of Lady sliced open and her insides laid out on a table.

"Enough of that kind of talk before dinner," Aunt Sarah says.

She ushers us into the kitchen. In the twelve years I've been away nothing has changed. The rooster clock is where it was when I lived with them. The stove and refrigerator Uncle Frank bought Aunt Sarah all those years ago is outdated but immaculately clean. My face breaks into an enormous smile when I see the table set for five.

"Please, sit," Aunt Sarah says.

As soon as we are seated, she brings a pot of stew and a plate of cornbread to the table. "There's apple pie for dessert, so save room," she tells Jared.

Uncle Frank nods to Rebecca who is smiling from ear to ear.

"Heavenly Father, thank you for looking out for Lady, she's a good horse. We would be sad if she died, especially Aunt Kayla and Uncle Jared, so if you can, could you make her well again." Rebecca sneaks a sideways look at the two of us, unaware that Uncle Frank is watching. He clears his throat and her little face becomes serious again. "Oh, and thank you for the food we're about to eat and the hands that prepared it. Amen."

The pot of stew is passed around. While we fill our bowls, Rebecca grills me about Lady's surgery. She asks intelligent questions that impress Jared and me. Uncle Frank and Aunt Sarah don't act surprised. And why should they, they're the ones who encouraged her inquisitive mind.

"Did they really pull her insides out?" Rebecca asks, slipping the question past a spoonful of food and her mother.

Aunt Sarah's head snaps up. "That's enough. We don't talk about such things at the dinner table."

It's a shame Rebecca's eagerness to learn is thwarted by Aunt Sarah's desire for her to be more ladylike. Personally, I don't see anything wrong with the conversation. And judging by the smirk on Jared's face, he agrees.

"So, Rebecca, what do you do in your free time?" he asks.

Her face lights up. "I help dad with the cattle. Did I tell you he's teaching me to drive the tractor? Isn't that great?"

I see by the look Uncle Frank and Aunt Sarah share that there is disagreement between them about the tractor driving lessons. Instead of confronting the situation now, Aunt Sarah smiles fondly at Rebecca.

"Hurry up, dear, you still have homework to do and it's getting late." Turning to me she says, "Rebecca insisted on seeing you and Jared. By now she's usually done her homework and had her bath."

Rebecca makes a face and groans. "I don't need a bath. I had one yesterday."

Watching Rebecca brings back memories of my own childhood. When I was her age, I hated the b-word.

Uncle Frank chuckles. "She's a chip off the old block," he says. This observation brings a smile to Aunt Sarah's face. I assume he's talking about Rebecca taking after him. I soon learn I'm mistaken. "Rebecca is just like your Aunt Sarah when she was Rebecca's age. Sarah adored your grandfather. She followed him everywhere he went from morning until night before she started school. Your grandmother tried everything to take the tom boy out of her, didn't work though."

Aunt Sarah's face turns red. She gets up from the table and begins to clear the dishes. Over her shoulder she says, "Frank, your imagination is running amuck. Must be someone else you're remembering."

I excuse myself to help. As I gather the rest of the dishes from the table, I listen to Uncle Frank. "Your Mom punched me right in the nose when I was twelve, maybe thirteen years old.

All I said was she was sure pretty and someday I'd like to kiss her."

"And what did Mom say?" Rebecca asked in a giddy voice filled with laughter.

"She said she'd sooner kiss a donkey, so I grabbed her with the intention of planting a good one on her. She balled up her fist and hit me hard. I walked home from school with blood all over my shirt. When my dad heard what happened, he said I had it coming."

"He loves telling that story," Aunt Sarah says to me.

"Is it true?" I ask, setting the dishes on the countertop.

She chuckles and turns to look at me. There's a sparkle in her eyes. "It's true. What he doesn't know is that I liked him. I didn't want him to know, so I acted put out when he grabbed me. I had to do something, so I punched him."

We do the dishes in silence, Aunt Sarah washing, me drying. It isn't until she's wiping off the stovetop that she says, "Is there's anything going on between the two of you?"

Aunt Sarah catches me off guard. While I think of a reply, Rebecca comes in to kiss me goodnight. "Call me tomorrow to tell me how Lady is doing. Okay?" she says with childish enthusiasm.

I cup her face in my hands and smile down at her. "Of course I'll call you. And when Lady is well, you can come visit her. Okay?"

Rebecca's head bounces up and down. She kisses her mom and trots off to do her homework.

"Don't mess around, Rebecca," Aunt Sarah warns.

"I won't."

"And don't forget your prayers."

"Okay, Mom," she says as she scampers upstairs.

Aunt Sarah hangs her apron on a peg by the back door and turns to me. "That girl is a handful. God knew what he was doing when he gave us only one." She contemplates me a moment and smiles. "So, is there?"

"Is there what?"

"Don't pretend you forgot the question. What's up with you and Jared?"

I hang the dishtowel up and turn around. "He'd like there to be more than friendship but honestly, Aunt Sarah, I can't see us being anything more than what we are. Sometimes he makes me so mad...."

"Sounds like Brandon and Maggie when they were young. Brandon idolized your mom. The only way he could get her attention was to ruffles her feathers."

"That's about as smart as an ostrich hiding his head in the sand," I mutter on my way to the living room. Jared's cell phone rings, and I can tell by the look on his face it's not good.

"We'll be right there," he says. He snaps the case shut and picks up his hat from the sideboard. That's when he sees me standing in the doorway.

"It's Lady. She's taken a turn for the worse," he says, taking me by the arm.

There's no time to say goodbye. I grab my coat off the hook by the door and run after Jared.

J. B. Williams

Chapter 12

Jared breaks every speed limit. Twenty minutes later we ring the after hour bell at the clinic. A woman wearing green surgical scrubs answers the door. She introduces herself as Rene, the night nurse taking care of Lady.

"Thad wants you in there," she says, and I follow her.

I feel awful it's me going in to see Lady when Jared is so visibly upset. Seeing him this way makes me realize underneath his tough exterior is a soft heart. I guess he's no different from other men I've met. Like them, Jared finds it difficult to show his emotions.

I've been through the procedure hundreds of times, even so my knees go weak when I see Lady suspended from the ceiling in a canvas sling. Her coat is dull and lifeless. She stares at me through vacant eyes that tell me she has given up. At the sound of my voice, Lady makes a grumbling noise that breaks my heart. Immediately my eyes tear up. Thad's back is to me. He turns around and comes toward me shaking his head.

"She's burning up. We're doing all we can. Got any ideas?"

I shake my head and blink back tears. I'm no longer a veterinarian. I'm a lover of horses, particularly this one. I lift Lady's chin to my shoulder so it's not dangling toward the floor. My fingers run through her tangled mane as I whisper, "You have to give it your best shot, girl. Please, for me." Overcome with grief, I rest my head against her neck and weep. This is when Thad leaves us alone so I can say goodbye. I am grateful for this opportunity to let my emotions flow freely. I don't have to pretend to be strong. My shoulders heave with convulsive sobs. I'm cried out when the door opens. I glance over my shoulder. The eyes above the mask are unmistakable. Thad has allowed Jared to be with Lady during her last hours.

We stand on either side of her. Jared tells Lady she is going to be all right. I can tell by the tremor in his voice he doesn't believe it.

I pray, silent at first. I don't recall when my words become audible.

Father, please intervene where medicine can't. You are the Creator and Giver of life. You know what's wrong with

Lady. Heal her, please. She's in so much pain, Father... I can't go on. Tears soak my face mask. In a tender moment Jared reaches under Lady's neck and takes my hand. We cling to one another and watch the monitoring devices and wait for the smallest sign Lady is fighting to survive.

We hardly notice when Thad comes in and lays a cooling blanket over Lady. He turns on a switch that forces cold water through the coils in the blanket. For the longest time he stands there in silence, watching the monitor. He shakes his head and leaves. Several minutes later he returns with another bag of antibiotics which he exchanges for the near empty one. Our eyes meet. He doesn't speak, but I know what he's thinking. With a temperature of 105, things don't look good. He pats my shoulder and walks to the chair near the door. With a sigh of resignation he collapses into the chair and crosses his arms over his chest. He leans his head against the wall and closes his eyes. I wonder if he's a praying man, or is he racking his brain for some miracle drug he might have missed?

"He's a good man," I whisper.

Jared looks over Lady's neck at Thad. "He sure is. The clinic is lucky to have him."

Eventually Jared changes places with Thad. I don't know how men do it. Jared drifts off to sleep sitting upright in the chair. His head bobs only a couple of times before his chin drops to his chest. I'm exhausted, but I refuse Thad's advice when he suggests it might be a good idea if I catch a few hours of sleep on the couch in the reception area. The thought Lady might die alone without someone stroking her forehead and telling her how much she is loved is unthinkable. Nonetheless, I must have dozed off standing up. When Thad touches my shoulder, my eyes fly open. He's smiling and pointing to the monitor. Lady's temperature has dropped to 103. Normal for a horse is 101. When I speak her name, she acknowledges my presence with a small whinny that awakens Jared. In an instant he's beside me, glancing at the monitor. His tentative smile broadens.

"Her temperature is dropping. That's a good sign, isn't it?" He gives Thad and me an anxious glance.

"Yes, it's a good sign." His eyes brighten with newfound hope I quickly squelch by adding, "But she's not out of the woods yet. She's still very sick."

The light in his eyes dies like a flickering candle.

"But we aren't giving up, are we, Lady?" I say, patting her face.

Lady shakes her head. The three of us share an optimistic laugh and lavish praise upon her for agreeing to put more effort into her recovery. Our little talk with her must work. By mid-morning the glazed look in Lady's eyes is gone. She's alert. Thad and I agree she is past the crisis although the road to recovery will be a long one.

"If there are no more complications, she can go home in a week to ten days. While she's here, you guys can come around as often as you like." Thad maneuvers Jared and me to the door and opens it. "Now, I insist the two of you go home and get some rest."

Jared offers Thad his hand. "You're a good man. A simple thank you doesn't seem enough under the circumstances."

There's a twinkle in Thad's eye. "Hopefully you won't change your mind when you get my bill."

We are on our way to the truck when Jared and I turn to see Thad running toward us. "Her gut works," Thad says. "My guess is the two of you leaving made her nervous. You weren't out the door more than a minute when she defecated. Just a little bit, but it's a start."

Jared shakes Thad's hand and then for good measure, wraps him in a manly hug that surprises me. I don't think I've ever seen Jared quite so animated or demonstrative, especially with another man. Jared catches himself. His face turns red and he releases Thad and turns to me.

"Did you hear that, Lady's innards are working?"

"I did. That's great news." Out of gratitude I go to Thad and offer him my hand. He's either blind or forward. He wraps me in a hug, something I wouldn't expect from someone I hardly know. I wait a second or two so I don't appear stiff and unappreciative before pulling out of his arms. He chuckles and lowers his arms with an apologetic smile. There's nothing in his eyes to suggest he meant more than what happened—a friendly hug of enthusiasm.

"Thanks again, Thad," I say and walk toward the truck.

Jared's face is one big smile when he slides in beside me. He glances sideways and says, "Thad's an okay guy, don't you think?"

"Yes, he's a good vet."

The motor comes to life. Jared backs the truck out of the parking space and pulls onto the main road leading home. We don't talk which is nice for a change. I stare out the window at the passing countryside. Montana is beautiful in the fall. The leaves are a multitude of colors ranging from bright red to shades of orange, gold and deep purple. I smile at the squirrels scampering through the fallen leaves in search of nuts to store for winter. I'm thinking about Thad when Jared's voice shatters the stillness.

"Is there something about him you don't like?"

I turn to look at him in dismay. "What?"

"You don't like Thad, do you?"

I give his ludicrous statement a moment's thought.

He's baiting me to see if I'm attracted to Thad.

I reply, tongue in cheek, "Of course I like him. What's not to like? He's good looking, we have a lot in common, and you did say you thought a vet in the family would be a good thing."

It's plain to see he doesn't know whether I'm teasing or not. Lines furrow his brow. He studies me for a moment before returning his attention to the road ahead. I'm having a silent chuckle over his reaction and the look on his face. When he stops at the mailbox on the side of the road near the gate leading into the ranch, I hop out and gather up two day's worth of mail. Without glancing at him I get into the truck and fasten my seatbelt. As we bounce along the road toward home, I thumb through several advertisements until I come to a letter from Mom.

Jared stops the truck in front of the house and gets out. I follow him into the foyer where I drop all the mail, except Mom's letter, on the credenza in the hall and walk toward the staircase with the intention of taking a hot shower and falling into bed. As I mount the first stair, I remind myself to call Nathan in the morning to arrange to meet him in town for dinner. I also want to stop in to see Lady on the way.

"Do you want to tell me what that was all about?" Jared's rich baritone voice echoes off the vaulted ceilings.

I hesitate and turn around on the bottom step. There's no point in acting like I don't know what he's talking about. We stare at each other a moment, then I give him a tired smile. "If you want to know something, especially if it concerns my feelings for someone of the opposite sex, come out and ask. Don't pussy foot around and expect me to take you serious. To answer your question, I find Thad a bit forward but that might change if I choose to know him."

Without waiting for a reply I mount the stairs. It's late. My legs feel like butter, and the beginning of a headache is crawling up the back of my neck. Getting into a verbal battle with Jared would only make it worse.

One look in the mirror and I shudder. My auburn hair is dull and lifeless and in need of a good wash. I lean toward the mirror for a better look and question why any man would find me attractive, especially after the long hours of keeping watch over Lady. The dark circles beneath my eyes make me look old and worn well beyond my years. I unbuckle my belt, drop my jeans to the floor and pull my shirt over my head. I glance in the mirror and chuckle. Static electricity makes my hair stand on end.

I take a long, hot shower while mulling over the day's events. Hardly something I will forget. Nearly losing Lady confirms my decision to stay in Montana.

Besides, mom is getting older. She needs me. Following that thought there's another. *Who am I kidding? It's Laura.*

The following morning I open my eyes to gray skies peeking through the curtains. As I become fully cognizant, silence greets me along with a cold chill that tells me Jared forgot to turn up the heat before leaving the house. I glance at the clock on the nightstand. It's after eight. Even so, my body resists the idea of getting up. Ten minutes later I contemplate tossing the covers aside. Five minutes after that, I actually do.

Instead of getting dressed, I pull on a robe and stuff my feet into slippers. I arrive in the kitchen and stop in the open doorway. Derek and Jared are seated at the table reading the newspaper.

I say the first thing that pops into my head. "What are you two doing?"

The two of them lower their newspapers. They stare at me for a long moment and then burst into laughter. I know exactly what's tickling their funny bones and try to tame my hair. I wish I'd taken time to at least run a brush through it.

"You look like Cheshire Cats grinning like that," I mutter on the way to the coffee pot. When I turn around they are still smiling. To qualify my appearance, I add, "I didn't know anyone was here."

"We're just having fun with you," Derek says, laying the paper aside.

He isn't wearing work clothes, which surprises me. It also sends up a red flag. "I thought you were coming back to work today?" I ask, trying to keep my voice nonchalant.

Jared's eyes rest on Derek for an answer to my question, the second sign something is going on.

Derek smiles and stands; he pulls out a chair for me and nods for me to take a seat. I do as he says and look up at him with uncertainty. "What's going on?"

He sits beside me and clears his throat. I'm getting an uneasy feeling in the pit of my stomach. I'm not a patient person in circumstances such as this. "Spit it out, Derek. Just say what's on your mind. Please."

"I gave notice to Jared this morning."

"Notice about what?"

Derek clears his throat. His eyes hold mine. "I've been offered a position with a small church in Missouri while I attend seminary. It's an answer to prayer."

It's too early in the morning for news like this. My eyes fill. With trembling lips I try to speak. "But...but, are you sure this is what you want?" I look from Derek to Jared and then I stand up and walk to the counter to refill my coffee cup. At this distance I feel less likely to throw my arms around Derek and beg him to stay. Now more than ever I need him to be here. But I don't tell him because I can't ask him to give up his dream just to play big brother. I pull myself together and smile.

"I'm going to miss you," I say, cutting off whatever it was he was about to say.

The light leaves his eyes for a moment and I realize he was going to ask me to go with him. Instead, the chair legs scrape the floor and echo our goodbye as he pushes away from the table.

"So, when are you leaving?"

"Sunday. Right after church."

His eyes rest on mine for a moment and then he smiles and opens his arms. I walk into them, rest my cheek on his chest and remember the days we traveled the rodeo circuit together. I recall our first kiss and the confusion that followed. I had a childish crush on Derek then, now I'm not sure what I feel for him. Until I'm certain of my feelings, I can't promise him anything. And I certainly can't ask him to put his life on hold for me.

"Keep in touch," I whisper and pull away.

I can't bear to look into his eyes, so I turn and walk away without looking back.

All this time Jared sits in silence.

I hate saying goodbye, so I excuse myself and mount the stairs in tears.

Chapter 13

From my bedroom window I see Derek's car disappear beyond the trees lining the driveway. I'm sad he's leaving, but I'm also a bit envious. He's grown spiritually while I've ignored that part of my life. It isn't that I didn't go to church in California. I did, almost every Sunday, unless an emergency came up at the clinic. I belonged to the singles group Bible study, too, so I have head knowledge; it's the faith part I struggle with on a daily basis.

I dress quickly and pick up the phone. Nathan's voice mail invites me to leave a message.

"Nathan, one of the horses had emergency surgery yesterday. I want to sit with her today. I was hoping we could meet in town, somewhere casual because I'll be wearing jeans and boots. I hope to leave within the hour so if you get this message, call me here at the ranch. Otherwise call me at the clinic since I left my cell phone in California. You know the place, the one down the road from the ranch—can't recall the name of it right now.

I'm applying moisture to my face when I hear the phone. On the third ring I realize Jared is not in the house, so I go to mom's room to answer.

"Hi, it's Nathan. Sorry to hear about your horse."

Funny, his voice hasn't changed since high school.

"She's recovering. It was touch and go for a while."

"How about meeting at McDonalds? Like old times."

If any other man made a date to meet at McDoanlds, I'd think of him as a skin flint, but I know Nathan better. He suggests McDonalds because of the memories we share. Odds are he'll be sitting in our booth when I get arrive.

"Sounds like a plan," I tell him. "See you around, let's say, five, five-thirty?"

"Perfect. Football practice gets over around four. I can shower and be there by five."

"Excellent. I'm looking forward to seeing you."

"Me, too," he says.

The phone clicks in my ear. With a shrug, I replace the phone in the cradle and hurry back to my room to put the final touches on hair and makeup. I check the time. Quarter to ten. In the hallway downstairs I stop long enough to pull on my jacket. It's a good thing I do because a cold wind takes my breath away as I step outside.

The Suburban is parked at the end of the walkway. A peek inside tells me Jared left the keys in the ignition. The leather seats are icy cold when I slide in. Rather than take the vehicle without checking with Jared first, I drive around the house to the front of the barn. I leave the engine running and go in search of him. On the way to the office I pass Lady's empty stall. Jared is immersed in finances, something he doesn't usually do unless prodded according to mom. Clearing my throat, I step inside where a space heater burns red hot in the corner. Jared's jacket hangs on a peg near the door. He's wearing a plaid shirt and jeans, and glances up at me.

"On your way to the clinic?" he asks. He rests his elbows on the desktop and twiddles the pencil between his fingers while his eyes check me out. He gives me an appreciative smile I pretend to ignore.

"Yes. Do you need the Suburban?"

"No. Why?"

"Well, I thought I'd meet Nathan for dinner."

He stops twirling the pencil. "Not a problem, I'll drive your mom's Mercedes."

"Oh. Okay." On the way out I say, "See you later."

"Yeah, later," he replies.

On the drive to the clinic I wonder where Jared is going tonight. He has a truck so it must be some place special to take the Mercedes. By the time I pull into the clinic parking lot my curiosity is conjuring up all sorts of scenarios. For starters, Jared has lousy taste in women if past history is taken into account.

That's not my problem.

Thad meets me at the door. He's on his way out and by the way he's dressed, I assume he's making a ranch call. His eyes brighten when he sees me.

"Hi, there, Lady's doing much better today. She'll be glad to see you."

We linger near the door a few minutes while Thad gives me the rundown on Lady's vitals. "Her temp is normal, she's had a good bowel movement, and she's being fed small amounts of grass hay several times a day. The sutures look good. So, unless something unforeseen happens, you can take her home next Wednesday."

Before getting in his truck, he calls over the hood. "I shouldn't be long, just a routine visit to check on a couple of broodmares. Lady is in a stall behind the clinic. By the way, do you want me to pick you up something for lunch?"

"Sure. That would be nice. Thanks," I say and walk around the building.

Lady is in a freshly bedded stall. She whinnies when I slide the door open. Before going inside, I read Thad's notes on her chart. She is to be hand walked a few minutes several times a day. According to the chart, she was walked at eight o'clock this morning. While I'm reading, the nurse from yesterday walks by and smiles at me.

"You can take her for her mid-morning walk if you'd like. Just keep her on the rubber mats so she doesn't slip."

I nod and reach for Lady's halter hanging on the wall. I see no reason to tell the nurse I know the importance of after surgery procedures. Lady puts her nose in the halter, eager to go somewhere. She walks slowly and steps over the threshold of the stall with care. It's obvious she is in a great deal of pain, but she ignores it and walks alongside me. As we walk, I tell her how proud I am of her and how much I love her. A lump forms in my throat when I think we might have lost her had it not been for Thad's expertise in surgery.

The nurse walks by again. She stops and ponders Lady a minute. "You know what, if she feels up to it, there's a sunny area at the end of the barn. There might even be a few blades of grass left from summer. When Thad gets back, I'll tell him you and Lady are there."

At the end of the barn I find a picnic table. Beneath it, and surrounding it for about a twenty foot square, is dried grass. Down the length of the barn sunflowers grow, some so tall they reach the eaves of the barn. There are several pipe corrals nearby where horses not as sick as Lady are out for some exercise. The backdrop behind all of this takes my breath away. Mountains capped with snow rise several thousand feet into an unusually blue sky for this time of year.

Lady is at the end of the lead rope munching grass when Thad comes toward us carrying two brown bags. I'd have to be blind not to notice his muscular frame. He has a nice smile, too. I recall yesterday when he hugged me. I may have read him all wrong. Certainly Jared is a good judge of character, and if he likes him, maybe I shouldn't be so judgmental. Thad hands me a bag with a soft drink and a sandwich.

"I hope you like roast beef."

Ten minutes later we're talking like old friends comparing notes about college and vet school. Thad studied in Nebraska. His first choice was The University of Davis, my alma mater, but he couldn't get in. Pity, we would have been in the same graduating class. Thad takes a bite of sandwich and nods to Lady. "She's a great horse. Why don't you breed her again before it's too late? If she were mine, I'd have a whole herd of her offspring."

"Until Brandon died I didn't intend to move back. Jared kind of took her over."

Thad laughs. "Then take her back—unless you plan on returning to California." He wrinkles his brow and adds, "Even if you did go back, there are plenty of people out there who would give their eye teeth to own a foal out of her."

"You're probably right. Reining horses are hot right now, and Lady has some very good reining horses in her pedigree."

We eat the rest of our lunch in silence. Then Thad gets up and wads his bag into a ball and tosses it into the garbage can nearby. He contemplates me a moment. "You should probably walk her a bit more and then take her back to her stall. How long are you going to be here?"

"Four-thirty; I have a dinner date at five."

I pull Lady's head out of the grass and lead her toward her stall. We are careful to stay on the rubber mats as we follow Thad. He steps aside and watches me take Lady into the stall. Before walking away, he says, "If you get bored in there, I'm scheduled for surgery in about twenty minutes. I could use another hand."

I give him a contemplative look and say, "I'll think about it."

No pressure, he turns and leaves.

My fingers are itching to go back to work. It doesn't take me long to make up my mind. I give Lady a pat and tell her I'll be back to take her for later. Lady doesn't seem to care if I stay or go. She's standing in the corner of the stall, nose to the soft bedding, snoring.

When I arrive in the scrub room, Thad is washing up. He smiles and nods to the soap. Standing side-by-side we make sure our hands and arms are disinfected and then slip into scrubs, booties, caps, masks and finally latex gloves. The patient is a Shetland pony, two years of age. His testicles never dropped, which is a serious situation if the cords to the testicles become entangled around the intestines.

The pony is on its side with his hind leg tied up to allow Thad room to cut into the empty sack and thus have access to the area where he assumes the testicles are. I act as his assistant, handing him what he needs. Beads of sweat shine on Thad's forehead. He works quickly, probing with his fingers until he finds what he's looking for. He pulls the first testicle out and snips it off.

"Clamp," he says, and I apply the clamp.

There's very little blood. When he exposes the second testicle, my mouth drops open. It's the size of an apple and takes a bit of doing to pull it out through the incision. Thad snips it from the cord and I apply the clamp.

He smiles at me above the mask. "Want to finish up?"

Thad doesn't wait for my reply. He backs out of the surgery room and smiles at me through the window. I nod to the nurse. She hands me a pre-strung needle. I put a stitch in the cords and then concentrate on the access opening. I leave one stitch out so the area can drain. The pony's leg is released, and he is slowly removed from the inhalant anesthesia and starts to breath on his own. Soon his eyes open. He's groggy, but while in this state, the surgery table is lowered to the floor. All vitals are good, so I leave him in the care of the nurse in charge.

Thad is in his office when I come out of the scrub room. He looks up from his file and smiles. "I talked with Morton, the senior vet. He's on vacation in Hawaii. He'd like to talk to you about joining us when he gets back."

I lean on the door frame and smile. If Thad thinks he pulled one over on me, he's dumber than I thought. But that's not what I say. I play along with him.

"It's something to think about," I tell him.

The clock on the credenza behind his desk reads three-thirty. If I want to walk Lady again before I leave, I'll have to hurry.

"Thanks for the fun afternoon," I say and wander down the hall.

When I get to the door that leads outside, I look over my shoulder. Thad is at the front desk talking to the night nurse, probably giving her instructions on the newest surgery case.

Lady greets me with enthusiasm. An afternoon nap agrees with her. I slip her halter on and take her outside. She moves in slow, painful steps, ten times down the matted walkway. Then I reward her with fifteen minutes of non stop grass eating. Tomorrow and the days after will be slim pickings because there is no grass left. As the sun sets, a cold breeze causes me to draw the zipper of my jacket up. Clouds gather over the distant mountain tops. In another hour it will be dark. No matter how sore her stomach is Lady objects when I pull her head up and lead her toward her stall. After adjusting the belly band that covers the staples that hold the incision together, I pat her muscular neck and tell her goodbye. She ignores me and dives into the small ration of hay in her feeding bin.

I stop in the restroom to redo my makeup and run a brush through my hair. On the way to the Suburban, I stop at the desk to tell the receptionist I'm leaving.

"Tell Thad I will be here in the morning," I add on my way out the door.

Thad's truck isn't in the parking lot. But that's not unusual for a veterinarian on call. I expect he will be in and out all night.

On my way to meet Nathan, I ponder the day's events. It felt good to assist in surgery. I've missed the challenges associated with emergencies such as the one today. Thad's offer sends a tingle of excitement up my spine.

As long as I'm staying in Montana I might as well work with Thad. The clinic is close to home, clean and offers state of the art equipment. What more can a vet ask for?

Chapter 14

Just as I thought. Nathan is sitting in our favorite booth when I arrive. He smiles and waves at me as I walk past the plate glass window. I feel like sixteen again as I push through the door. While sitting down, I give him a prolonged glance. The past twelve years have been good to him. Although his blond hair has receded a bit, his eyes are still the same vibrant blue. I slide into the booth opposite him.

"Hope you don't mind, but I ordered for us. Big Macs, fries and a soda just like the old days," he says.

I shake my head and remove my jacket, laying it beside me. The place is just as I remember it, except they now have a children's area with slides and plastic tubing for the little ones to crawl through. The door to the play area is closed. Even so, the noise of screaming children is audible.

The booths are the same color; the same pictures hang upon the walls. Even the tile flooring is the same. It's kind of like coming home.

When I verbalize this to Nathan, he chuckles.

"So, how have you been?" I ask. This is as good a place to start as any.

"I've been okay. Actually, I've been doing very well. Last year I made head coach of the football team. We had a 10-1 record. A couple more years like that and I might get noticed by one of the top ten colleges."

I slant my head and study him for a moment. "Is that what you want, to coach college football?"

His eyes light up with the thought it might actually happen. "Doesn't every coach want a job like that?"

I don't follow college football, however, I do watch pro football, and I have to admit I get caught up in all the hoopla.

"I'd have thought you might set your sights on professional football."

Nathan shakes his head. "College football is more exciting."

I don't have time to ask him to explain. Our number is called. Nathan stands and ambles to the counter. I hear him say, "Thanks." He carries the tray to the condiment area and grabs a fistful of ketchup, then goes to the drink dispenser to fill two paper cups with Pepsi—one regular, one diet. When he returns, he sets our dinner out and returns the tray to the counter. On his way back, he stops to talk to a group of young men, football players I assume. Manly laughter erupts after one of the boys glances my way. Nathan's cheeks turn bright red. When he returns to the booth, curiosity gets the best of me. "Are they giving you a hard time about me?"

Nathan dips a French fry in Ketchup and stuffs it in his mouth. Some things never change. Nathan's love of French fries is one of them. He chews and swallows, and then he answers my question. "He wanted to know who the hot redhead was and if Angie knew I was cheating on her?"

Nathan didn't mention anything about a woman in his life at the luncheon after the funeral, so this comes as a bit of a shock. I take a bite of my Big Mac and wait for an explanation as to why he asked me out to dinner if he's seeing someone. When this doesn't happen, I ask the inevitable question.

"So, aren't you going to tell me about Angie?"

Nathan's cheeks turn red. "She wants to get married, and I don't. We've been dating for a couple of years. I want to make a name for myself before I settle down with a wife and kids."

There is an edge to his voice that says he doesn't want to discuss this topic. He takes a huge bite of his hamburger and stares at me a moment.

"So, what have you been up to?"

I finish chewing and swallow. "Let's see. Well, I helped save a Shetland pony's life today. His testicles didn't drop. Lucky for the pony Thad dropped by to see one of the other animals on the farm and noticed the pony. When he inquired as to the sex, the rancher told him he was still a stallion. Thad then asked when they were going to castrate the pony" I take another bite and chew. Nathan urges me on with a smile. I swallow and continue. "The owner told him the pony's testicles hadn't dropped yet, so Thad insisted on examining the Shetland. Then he told them the pony had to be gelded immediately. During the operation Thad found what he expected, the cords were wrapped around the pony's intestines. The pony would have strangled if Thad hadn't performed surgery."

Nathan's Pepsi goes down the wrong tube. He chokes and sputters, and when he recovers he says, "Thanks for sharing. If you don't mind that's a bit more information than I care to digest along with my food."

I break into laughter at the disgusted look on Nathan's face.

"Sorry, I didn't mean to spoil your dinner. Vets don't let stuff like that bother them. We go from one surgery to the next while munching a sandwich. If we wait until we have time to sit down and enjoy lunch, we starve."

Nathan gives me a crooked smile and asks, "Who is this Thad guy anyway?"

As I fill Nathan in on the newest member at the clinic, he begins to smile. I'm talking a mile a minute when I stop abruptly and raise an amused brow.

"What?" I ask.

"You should hear yourself. You're talking like a member of the staff even though you haven't accepted the position yet."

Nathan pokes another fry into his mouth.

"Well, if I'm staying, I have to work. And offers like this don't come around every day, you know."

Nathan's eyes twinkle with mischief. "And they don't come with a handsome veterinarian mixed into the bargain, right?"

Color floods my cheeks. "I have no romantic interest in Thad, if that's what you mean. We hardly know one another. Besides, I don't date co-workers. It makes for a sticky situation at best."

We are having a good laugh when a woman walks in. Nathan's eyes shift to her as she stands at the counter. My gaze follows his. She is in her late twenties, tall, muscular, not particularly attractive—very masculine to my way of thinking.

Long black hair is gathered into a pony tail. She's wearing a tight, form-fitting tank top, tights and tennis shoes.

"That's Angie," he says.

One of the young men at the table glances our way and smiles. It doesn't take a rocket scientist to figure out one of them called Nathan's girlfriend. And they are having a great old time waiting for the fireworks.

Angie turns around and stares at us. I shift my eyes back to Nathan. We're adults, and I'm happy to see that he waves her over to us. Angie smiles and walks toward us. Nathan stands and waits for her to be seated to introduce us.

"You remember me telling you about Kayla, don't you?" Nathan asks.

Angie's eyes brighten. She smiles and offers me her hand across the table. I'm certain this gesture ruins the fun for the young men at the other table.

"Nice to meet you," I say.

Angie's handshake doesn't disappoint. Strong and firm, it goes with her physique. Her eyes hold mine—woman to woman we come to an understanding where Nathan is concerned.

Her lips curl into a smile. "Nathan has told me so much about you."

I like her immediately.

When Angie's number is called, Nathan leaves to pick up her order. Angie takes this opportunity to apologize for her little brother who is seated with the other jocks. Her eyes connect with his, and she takes him down a notch with a glance.

"Chuck didn't know Nathan had told me he was meeting you here," she explains while balling her fist up at him. Angie turns to me and grins. "I played along with his plan just to teach him a lesson." She studies me for a few seconds. "Besides, I wanted to meet you and see what you were like." Angie looks at the rowdy bunch of boys at the table and smiles. "Chuck called you a hot redhead."

Now we're both laughing at Chuck. His cheeks are bright red. He's taking a beating from his fellow football players. One of them speaks loud enough for Angie and me to overhear.

"What's a matter, little bro? Afraid sis will kick your booty when you get home?"

The laughter gets out of hand until Nathan stops beside their table. Immediately the boys' faces get serious. Moment's later they pick up the mess at the table and leave quietly. Nathan, Angie and I watch as the boys pile into cars and speed off.

Then Angie turns to Nathan. "So, what did you say to them?"

Nathan slides into the booth beside her and grins. "I told them I changed Saturday practice time to six a.m., and that every time they pull a stunt like this, I'll schedule it an hour earlier."

I have to admit that seeing the two of them together like this makes me want to have someone to share my life with. Whether Nathan admits it or not, Angie is firmly ensconced in his future.

They're perfect for one another.

With a sigh I reach for my jacket.

Nathan reacts by standing to give me a hand out of the booth. "You don't have to go yet, do you? I thought the three of us might take in a movie."

Angie is on her feet too. Her face lights up in a genuine smile. I know she means what she says. "It would be fun, how about it?"

"I have an early day tomorrow but thanks anyway. We'll do it another time." I offer Angie my hand and nod toward Nathan. "Take care of this big lug." My eyes find Nathan's. In those few seconds I see the boy instead of the man. "She's a keeper. Hang on to her."

With those words of wisdom I pull on my jacket and walk out the door. I don't look back. I cross the parking lot to the Suburban and start the motor.

When I arrive home, Jared is in the den watching the news. He looks over his shoulder and smiles. "How was dinner?"

I plop in the overstuffed chair. "We ate at McDonalds, kind of a reunion of past and present."

Jared doesn't make fun of the place or the reasoning behind it. He surprises me by remaining silent.

"I met Nathan's girlfriend. She's very nice and so perfect for him."

Jared leans forward and turns the volume down with the remote. "And?"

With a loud sigh I settle back into the folds of the chair. "And I'm jealous of their relationship."

Jared studies me for a few seconds. "Everyone is settling down. Clara and Bryan, Nathan and …"

"Angie."

"Nathan and Angie, and you feel like you're missing out on something, right?"

This new Jared has me spinning. I'm not sure what to make of him. Where once he had trouble relating to my feelings, he seems to understand where I'm coming from.

I raise my eyes and smile with embarrassment. "I know it's a sin to be envious of another person, but I am envious, and it would be a bigger sin not to admit it."

Jared chuckles as he pushes himself out of the chair. He walks across the room in long, lazy strides and picks up a log and tosses it in the fire. As if mesmerized by the amber flames, he stands there for a few moments before turning around.

A smile lingers on his lips.

"Well, since you're being truthful..." His face turns serious as his eyes hold mine. "I don't like Thad. I told you I did to see your reaction."

I'm dumbfounded. The room is very quiet as Jared waits for my reply.

"So, what's not to like?" I finally ask.

Our eyes meet lock on one another a few seconds. I certainly don't expect the response I get.

"He's got an ego the size of the Grand Canyon. And he's cocky." Jared comes toward me and stops. He stares down at me and breathes out a sigh. "I'm trying to give you space, Kayla, but if Thad shows a romantic interest in you, I will do everything within my power to convince you we are meant to be together."

I'm at a loss for words.

Jared leaves the room. Moments later I hear him set the house alarm and tromp up the stairs.

Chapter 15

The scent of burning wood and firelight gives the room a cozy feeling. I pull my chair closer to the fire and ponder the day's events; from surgery, to meeting Nathan, to Jared's final words before departing the room. The more I think about what he said, the angrier I become.

Of all the egotistical men, you take the prize. What makes you think I could ever be romantically involved with you?

I hear the shower upstairs and realize I am free to go up to my bedroom without another confrontation with Jared. My body aches as I push myself out of the chair and limp across the polished hardwood floor to the fireplace. I close the glass doors and tip toe up the stairs and down the hallway to my bedroom. Behind closed doors, I breathe a sigh of relief. Rather than meet

Jared in the hallway on my way to the other bathroom, I wipe my face with a tissue soaked in hand lotion and undress and crawl into bed.

Sleep doesn't come easy. In the darkness I confront my feelings. Even though I say otherwise, I don't want to be alone in old age. Yet, I don't want to commit to someone either. Commitment means answering to another human being, to accept the fact that my happiness depend upon someone who might let me down. That theory is immediately dashed to bits when Clara and Bryan creep into my thoughts. They are happily married with children, and as far as I know they combine careers with marriage and do it very well. Then I envision Nathan and Angie. It won't be long before the two of them get married and settle down behind the proverbial white picket fence.

Then I do the unthinkable. I compare Jared and Thad and decide I can't trust either of them. This feeling comes from a broken relationship I had a few years ago. Tears well in my eyes just thinking about the night Tim told me he thought we should see other people. He broke my heart like a piece of fine china tossed on the floor. To make matters worse, I hated myself for giving in to his demands for sex. When he walked out the door, a piece of me went with him. To heap salt upon my wounded heart, I learned later he had been seeing someone else for several weeks before breaking up with me. The only thing I'm grateful for is that I didn't get pregnant.

The door across the hallway opens and closes. Finally, the house is quiet. I'm nearly asleep when the phone shatters the silence. I hear Jared's muffled voice. Several minutes later a knock on my door brings me to a sitting position, heart racing.

I call out, "Jared, is that you?"

"Yes, can I come in?"

I reach for the robe at the end of my bed and stuff my feet into slippers. When I open the door, he's dressed in jeans, boots and a flannel shirt. "That was Tommy, the kid I hired to take care of the horses. The old mare is getting ready to foal. Tommy says there's only one leg showing and he thinks it's a hind leg at that."

"Call Thad," I say in a panic.

Jared shakes his head. "Thad isn't on call tonight. The guy who is on call has an emergency. He can't get here for a couple of hours. She'll be dead by then."

The old mare Jared refers to is the ranch matriarch, Lady's mother. Normally mares don't foal in November, but Zipper was hard to get in foal. Rather than lose a season with her, Jared continued to breed her until she finally took. I see fear in his eyes and know what he's thinking. If Zipper were younger she might make it, but she's twenty–two. Delivering a breech foal might kill her.

He turns and runs down the hallway.

I call after him. "I'll be there in a few minutes. Gather what you think I might need."

I'm dressed and pulling boots on when the thought occurs to me: I haven't delivered a breech foal in years.

When I arrive in the barn, all the lights are on. Jared stands in front of a stall near the end. Beside him is a pail of steaming water and clean rags. What I see when I peer into the stall makes my stomach roll. Zipper is wringing wet. She is shaking and her hind quarters are facing us. A hind leg is protruding from her swollen vulva. She grunts with the force of a contraction that does nothing because somewhere inside her the foal's other leg is hung up. I wash my hands and then drop to my knees behind Zipper. Speaking softly, I reach up inside her to locate the other foot. Several seconds pass. I find the tiny hoof and cup my hand around it so that when I free it from the pelvic area, the hoof doesn't perforate the rectum.

The next contraction squeezes my arm so tight I can't feel my fingers.

"Easy, girl, don't break my arm," I tell Zipper.

Zipper raises her head and gives me a pathetic look that begs me to do something.

The contraction eases and I work fast to free the foot. Once the foot is free, I ease it out of Zipper and wait for the next contraction. When it comes, I say, "Give it your all, old girl. Your baby is almost here."

The foal slides out on a gush of water, and I, along with Zipper, breath a sigh of relief. When she is able, Zipper lifts her head to see her new son. Her eyes are no longer filled with pain. After a quick examination of Zipper's heart rate, I step out of the stall to stand beside Jared. From there we watch the colt struggle to his feet, a necessary action to break the umbilical cord. It takes several attempts with a lot of vocal encouragement from Zipper before her son finally stands on wobbly legs. Shortly thereafter, Zipper grunts and gets up. She nuzzles her new son and begins the process of imprinting him. While all this is going on, I fill a syringe with Iodine to treat the umbilical stump. Once I've assured myself that mother and son are fine, I retreat to the aisle where Jared is waiting.

He drops an arm around my shoulder and pulls me to him. Exhaustion takes its toll. I rest my head against him and the two of us watch mother and son get to know one another.

His voice is a whisper when he looks down at me. "I've seen plenty of births but each time it's a miracle...especially this one. If you hadn't been here the colt would have died, maybe Zipper too."

An hour later we walk back to the house, confident mare and baby are going to be all right. Jared makes hot chocolate and we sit at the kitchen table. He stares at me and smiles.

"What?" I ask.

Reaching across the table, he pulls a piece of bedding straw from my hair. The tenderness in his eyes sends tiny impulses to my brain and immediately my guard goes up. I lean away from his fingertips and sip my hot chocolate. I'm afraid if I allow myself to respond to his kindness he'll read more into it than is intended. So, I look away to diffuse the connection between us. When I'm sure my emotions are under control, I look up. He's watching me.

"You're beautiful without makeup, do you know that?" he asks.

All my defenses shatter. Feminine instincts kick in. As if they have a will of their own, my eye lashes flutter flirtatiously; my lips curl into a teasing smile.

In my best Southern accent, I say, "Why, Mr. McChesney, are you toying with my emotions?"

He lowers his voice and twirls an imaginary moustache. "Miss Roberts, I daresay you've caught me in the act."

Once we stop laughing I take my cup to the sink. Jared follows me. Our shoulders brush as we walk down the hall and again as we climb the stairs. He walks me to my bedroom and reaches past me to open the door. Before I have time to object, he lowers his lips to mine and kisses me so tenderly I don't want him to stop. And then, when our lips part, he just smiles and walks down the hallway while I stare after him with my mouth open.

In the kitchen the following morning I find a note written in Jared's handwriting propped against the salt and pepper shakers. I flip the folded piece of paper open.

Your breakfast is in the microwave. I'll be back by twelve. Wait for me. I have a surprise for you. While I'm gone, could you check on our newest arrival?

I find myself smiling as I think about the long-legged, chestnut colt I helped bring into the world last night. If Tommy hadn't made a late night check on Zipper, the outcome might have been different. Most likely Zipper and her son would have died. The thought sickens me, yet it reminds me of the power of a loving God.

In all circumstances give praise, the voice says.

Out loud I do just that. "Thank you God for intervening in what might have been a disastrous situation. You are a mighty and loving Father who cares for all creation."

I pour a cup of coffee and take the plate of scrambled eggs and sausage out of the microwave. To save time, I eat while reading my e-mails on the computer in the den.

The first message is from Roger. He and Jessie packed up my personal belongings and made arrangements with the clinic to do the same with my medical equipment. All of my possessions were sent via UPS and should arrive within the week. My eyes widen.

I decided to lease your place. Hope you don't mind. I sent first and last month's rent off to you yesterday. I proposed to Jessie and she accepted. Hope you can come to the wedding. Tentative date set for July of next year. In the meantime, I'll be batching it at your place. Jessie is firm about not living together before we're married. Talk with you soon. Roger

The last people I expect to marry one another are Jessie and Roger. They are polar opposites, just like me and Jared. On the heels of this thought I recall the night before.

You certainly didn't fight Jared's kiss. In fact you acted like a stupid school girl. Your mouth trailed after his as he backed away.

Heat sears my cheeks with the mental picture.

"Don't let all this coupling make you desperate," I say aloud and move on to the next email.

It's from Clara and Bryan. They are flying in for Thanksgiving and hope that we can get together.

The next one stops me cold. It's from Mom, dated a week ago.

Laura has agreed to come to America. Isn't that wonderful?. She finally explained her hesitation. She didn't want to leave the children. So like her to think of others before herself. Flight plans made. We arrive in Montana November 23rd, just in time for Thanksgiving. I can't wait for you to meet her. Sarah and Frank will join us. Please pick up a turkey and all the other things we'll need. Love you, Mom

I set aside my half eaten breakfast and look at the calendar hanging on the wall above the desk. It's the 19th of November. Where did the time go?

I send off a quick reply to Roger and Jessie congratulating them on their engagement and another note to Mom telling her we'll be waiting at the airport. None of the other emails are of importance, so I delete them and go upstairs to shower and dress. For the longest time I stand under the warm spray and let the myriad of thoughts flutter around in my head. Closing my eyes, I put pictures to these thoughts. I envision Laura as a tall, dark haired Barbie doll except there's a halo around her head. She walks toward me with the help of Mom and holds out her hand. She's wearing dark glasses and one of Mom's elegant, fur-lined coats over chocolate brown slacks and sweater.

I'm jealous and I haven't even met her yet.

Disgusted with myself, I turn off the water and towel dry. I brush my teeth, dress in jeans and sweatshirt. Then I run a brush through my hair in an effort to tame the wild curls reflected in the steamy bathroom mirror.

On the way out the back door, I grab a jacket just in case. The horse trailer is parked outside the barn. A quick peek tells me it is empty. I pass by Lady's stall and then stop and back up. She peers through the grid at me and greets me with a hearty whinny that brings Jared out of the office.

He smiles and says, "Surprise. Thad called early this morning and said she could come home because she had her own personal vet."

I'm delirious. Without waiting, I slide the stall door open and go inside. Lady nuzzles my chest with her upper lip and then searches my pockets for a treat. Laughing, I push her away and peek under her belly to check the staples that hold the incision closed. The area is free of infection. In fact, there is hardly any swelling at all.

Jared watches me from outside the stall. When I look over my shoulder, his eyes hold a tenderness that takes my breath away.

"She looks great, doesn't she?" he says, as he moves away from the door to allow me to come out.

We're so close I smell the faint scent of his aftershave, and even though I try, I can't take my eyes off his face. It's as if the air around me is being sucked into a giant vacuum. The beat of my heart quickens even though I bid it to stay calm and collected. While all of this is going on, Jared wets his lips and gathers me in his arms. I'm helpless to move away. Even if I could, I'm not sure I want to. I feel his hand in the small of my back bringing me closer. His other hand is behind my head. I close my eyes and melt against him.

I don't think about anything except the moment. Then, when my brain kicks in, I receive a message from my subconscious that clicks off like a ticker tape.

What... are... you... doing?

Suddenly I rear back and stare up at him with my mouth dangling open. Like a parrot, I mimic the thought out loud. "What... are... you...doing?"

Jared chuckles and holds me at arms' length. "I'm kissing you good morning. That should be obvious?"

As he walks away, I whisper, "Dear Lord, it can't be. We are polar opposites. We'd never make it."

J. B. Williams

Chapter 16

When Thad arrives to examine Zipper and her foal, Tommy and I attempt to corral the rambunctious colt, but he is having no part of human hands. Several times I manage to get my arms around his neck, Each time he lunges free and hides behind Zipper. After a few minutes of this aggravation, the old mare pins her son against the wall. Tommy closes in on the colt's hindquarters while I attempt to put a halter on him.

"Easy does it," I say, reaching out to allow him to smell my open hand. With flared nostrils, he throws himself into reverse and backs into Tommy. Panic fills the little critter's eyes. He sends out a shrill whinny meant to alert his mother that he is in trouble. But old Zipper is standing there with her eyes closed, half asleep, not minding one bit that we are about to halter her son. After a bit of a wrestling match, I get the halter on the colt. Then I fasten a lead rope to the halter. As if she knows the game is over, Zipper sidesteps away from the colt. With a little encouragement from Tommy and a gentle tug on the lead rope from me, we bring the frightened colt to the front of his mother. He cries out, and Zipper nuzzles him on the rump as if to tell him everything is okay, that he will survive being handled by the two-legged creatures.

The colt's eyes are enormous when Thad presses the stethoscope against his side to listen to his heart and lungs; more so when Thad injects him with tetanus antitoxin. It's all I can do to keep the colt from running me over. Thad checks Zipper to make sure all the afterbirth has been expelled. He gives her a tetanus shot too. Once he's satisfied mother and son are healthy, he and I stand outside the stall. From there we watch Tommy turn the colt loose. The colt darts off. As he does, he lets fly with his back hooves, narrowly missing Tommy, who jumps sideways.

"Feisty little bugger," he says and slams the stall door.

The three of us laugh at the colt. He is at it again, bounding around his mother like a wind-up toy. Old Zipper looks at him as if he's taken leave of his senses then closes her eyes. She doesn't make a sound until he latches on to a teat and clamps down a tad too hard. Zipper squeals and nips him on the butt.

"Good job delivering that one," Thad says as we walk toward Lady's stall. He goes in and checks her incision and then we walk to his truck. Thad hands me some clean belly bands, antiseptic scrub, a bottle of antibiotics and a supply of syringes. We are discussing Lady's exercise program when his cell phone plays The Star Spangled Banner. He gives me an apologetic smile and flips the intruder open. As he listens, a veil of concern sweeps across his face. He jots down an address and turns to me.

"I have to go," he says and slides into his truck. As he pulls away from the barn, he leans out the open window. "Don't take too long to let us know about our offer. They're running me ragged. Working seven days a week doesn't give me much time for a private life."

He winks and speeds off. Once Thad is gone, I call Sarah to leave a message that I will shop for Thanksgiving groceries. I'm surprised when she answers the phone.

"What are you doing home?" I ask.

Sarah laughs. "Not hi, how are you doing? Just, what are you doing home?"

"Sorry."

"I took a few days off to get the house in order for the holiday. What's up?"

"How'd you like to go shopping for Thanksgiving dinner?"

Dishes rattle in the background which tells me Aunt Sarah is busy loading the dishwasher. She probably has her day planned.

When she says, "That sounds like fun. What time?" I'm pleasantly surprised.

The task at hand doesn't seem so distasteful now that Aunt Sarah has agreed to go. My heart warms to the thought of spending time with her. More than once while growing up, her wisdom helped me through a difficult time. Besides, I'm anxious to get her opinion about Laura coming to live with us.

As I drive up, Aunt Sarah walks out the front door wearing a jacket, jeans and a knitted cap that tames an abundance of silvery curls which fall gently around her shoulders. Her cheeks are a rosy pink and her eyes sparkle with affection as she opens the door of the Suburban and slips inside.

She buckles in and turns to me. "It takes a miserable task like grocery shopping to get us together, but so what?"

Our laughter fills the inside of the vehicle. As I drive, Aunt Sarah and I reminisce about old times, a safe subject since there's nothing you can do about the past. When we run out of stuff to talk about, we're quiet for several minutes. Then both of us talk at once.

Smiling, I say, "You first."

"No, go ahead. What's on your mind?"

My cheeks warm at the thought of admitting I'm not comfortable with Mom's decision to bring someone into our home—especially a foreigner who is blind. I clear my throat again.

Aunt Sarah smiles and nods encouragement.

The words drag across my teeth as if speaking them will make me a bad person. "What do you think about Laura coming to stay with us?"

Aunt Sarah looks into my eyes. Her smile fades into a look of concern. She reaches over and pats my leg. "There's more than enough room in your mother's heart for someone in need, Kayla. The Bible tells us to help the unfortunate. You've been gone so long you haven't seen the change in your mother or Brandon when he was alive. Both of them gave their hearts to Jesus. When you do that, it means you live to serve others, not your own selfish desires."

"I know I'm just thinking of myself, but Mom and I haven't had much time together, not with college and my internship, and then I was offered a job..." My voice trails off. "It's just that..." I try again and fail.

"You're afraid having Laura here will interfere with your relationship with your mom, aren't you?"

I nod and look at her. She's shaking her head, smiling.

"Kayla, Kayla, no one will ever take your place in your mother's heart. You're her little girl. That's how Moms see it. Don't let jealousy stand in the way of supporting your mother in this." Aunt Sarah pats my leg again. "From what I hear, Laura is a wonderful young woman who loves the Lord."

I don't tell Aunt Sarah that's the problem. I'm afraid Laura will outshine me. Instead, I nod in agreement and stare at the taillights of the car ahead. When we reach the supermarket, we get out and each of us grabs a cart on the way into the store. Aunt Sarah shops like a Tasmanian devil, flying down aisles, grabbing this and that and talking a mile a minute. When her cart is full, she starts on mine.

In between sprints we talk.

"How are you and Jared getting along?" Aunt Sarah raises an amused brow.

My cheeks turn red.

"Ah, ha, there's something going on between the two of you. Isn't there?"

Her mouth forms a perfect O when she realizes she's right. "I told Frank, and he said I had rocks in my head." Aunt Sarah reaches up to the top shelf for corn starch and tosses the box in my cart. Her eyes hold mine until she wrings the truth out of me.

"He won't give up. He insists we were meant to be together." I sigh to make my point.

This small gesture doesn't fool her. Or me.

"And you don't have any feelings for him, right?" Aunt Sarah asks with a hint of sarcasm as she moves down the grocery aisle.

I trot after her. "I'm not sure how I feel. Sometimes he drives me nuts and other times he gives me goose bumps."

Aunt Sarah stops and turns to face me. She's wearing that `I told you so' look.

"Goose bumps are good," she announces.

Everyone within hearing distance turns to look at us. Elderly ladies smile, young women smirk at my embarrassment and men pretend they don't hear. I move closer to Aunt Sarah and whisper out of the corner of my mouth. "Please, Aunt Sarah, everyone is watching us."

She looks around and smiles at the curious faces. "Spicy lemon sauce, that's what gives her goose bumps," she explains.

"Yeah, they'll believe that like I'm Cinderella and you're my mean stepmother."

Aunt Sarah wraps an arm around my shoulder and kisses my cheek, which makes it all the harder to be mad at her. Together we walk to the front of the store and unload our shopping carts. I've never bought this much food before, and when the checker announces the grand total of two-hundred twenty-five dollars, my eyes fly open.

"It's a wonder anyone celebrates Thanksgiving," I grumble while writing out the check.

The bagger tries to act like he cares. He probably hears this same comment a hundred times a day and is immune to complaints. He does, however, ask if we want help out. I can tell by the look on his face he's hoping we say no, so I say, "Yes."

On the way home we talk about Derek's plans to become a pastor. That leads Aunt Sarah to remind me the ladies of the church are planning a going away tea after the Sunday service. She stops mid sentence. "You and Jared will be there, won't you?"

My defenses go up. Without thinking I say, "Jared and I are not a couple, remember that. I'll tell him about the tea."

The sharpness in my voice brings a frown to Aunt Sarah's face. She pinches her lips together and turns to me.

"You protest too much. Whether you admit it or not, you have feelings for Jared. Denying them won't make them go away."

Her eyes regard me fondly, and I remember the evenings Aunt Sarah and I sat on her front porch after dark. We talked about mom and dad's decision to file for divorce, a subject that caused me to break into tears on more than one occasion. When I did, she held me, and I would lay my head on her shoulder and cry. And when I was done crying, we'd go inside and sit in her cozy kitchen and drink hot chocolate with marshmallows floating on top.

Tears Sting my eyes, so I turn away to stare out the window. I've known it all along. The reason I'm afraid of commitment is because of my parents' failed marriage and because some jerk broke my heart. A commitment means letting myself love someone again. Aunt Sarah is right. From the day Jared and I met there has been something between us; indescribable to anyone who hasn't felt as if their lives were intrinsically intertwined with another human being. As I grow in faith, I begin to understand that God is in control. He doesn't make mistakes, and if I allow Him, he will lead me to my life partner. They key is to be open to his will.

With a sigh I turn to look at Aunt Sarah. She takes her eyes off the road for a minute and smiles at me. For good measure she reaches over and pats my hand. It's as if she reads my mind.

"Don't try to do God's work, Kayla. If you do, you'll miss all the joy and expectation of what He has in store for you."

I hear noise in the kitchen and toss aside the covers. With a groan of resentment at having to leave the warmth of my bed, I pull on a robe and plod down the hall to the bathroom. I glance in the mirror and make face at myself. My hair is standing on end. A brush does little to tame my wild tresses. On my way downstairs, I tell myself Jared deserves to see me at my worst. I enter the kitchen and pause for effect. He does a double take that bends me over with laughter and sets the mood for the rest of the morning. He makes me a pancake in the shape of a wicked witch. Then he pours green food coloring in my orange juice. He calls it witches brew when he sets it down in front of me.

I smile demurely up at him and bat my eyelashes. "You should see me on my better days if you think this is bad."

He chuckles and pours coffee in our cups. Once the silliness is over, he settles on a serious subject. "Your mother called yesterday while you and Sarah were out."

I glance up quickly and knit my eyebrows together. "Why didn't you leave me a note?"

He shrugs. "I got in late and you were already in bed."

Feeling foolish, I say, "So what did she want?"

"She found a surgeon. Seems Laura's doctor over there sent her files to this guy in the States, and he agreed to perform the surgery pending his examination."

When I have no comment, Jared gives me a thoughtful stare. "You're not thrilled about Laura coming here, are you?"

Our eyes meet. I see no reason to deny what I feel. Besides, Jared has always been able to see right through me.

"No, I'm not, and before you lecture me, let me remind you my mother is susceptible right now."

The laughter of a moment ago is gone. Jared's eyes narrow as he stares at me. He hesitates and then gets up from the table. He scrapes the leftovers into the trash compactor and takes his plate to the sink to rinse. His posture tells me he's upset. When he turns around, he stares at me as if he sees me from an entirely different perspective. On the way out of the kitchen he says, "Your mother finds joy in helping others, a trait you might emulate."

My mouth dangles open. Several seconds later it snaps shut with the realization that Jared is right. I rinse my dishes, put them in the dishwasher and go upstairs to dress for church. When I come down, the house is quiet. I go to the kitchen and peer out the back window. The Suburban is parked in front of the barn. Quickly, before I lose my nerve, I go in search of Jared and find him in the feed room mixing grain for Zipper and the colt.

Red faced, I come to a stop behind him.

He turns to face me. The muscles in his jaw tense.

"Sorry I came on so strong."

"No, you are right."

Pail in one hand, he moves toward me. The beginning of a smile washes away the sadness on his face. We walk down the aisle to Zipper's stall, not saying anything. Jared pours the grain into the feeder inside the stall and closes the access door. He checks his watch and sits the pail on the ground.

Taking my hand, he says, "We'd better hurry. We'll be late for church."

On the way to church, Jared tells me the reason for his late homecoming the night before. Several of the men from church gathered with Derek to pray for him. After the prayer service, they had dinner.

"He's one heck of a guy. I only wish I hadn't been blind to his calling. There were times I asked him to work Sundays so I could go skiing or ride in a rodeo, and Derek never complained."

Jared's confession sends a flood of warmth over me. The voice inside my head speaks loud and clear.

Trust me, child, this is the one.

J. B. Williams

Chapter 17

The Bible tells us to love one another. We've all heard the saying, 'Remove the log from your own eye before pointing out a speck in someone else's eye'. Then there's the commandment that tells us not to covet or allow jealousy to rule our hearts. If these are the criterion by which God judges, I'm in trouble.

Jared's voice breaks the quiet. "A penny for your thoughts." I look at him and he frowns. "What is it?"

I blow out a breath and say, "I'm not a very nice person, so why does God care?"

Jared chuckles as if he knows exactly how I feel. But it's what he says that leaves me speechless. "God loves us in spite of ourselves, Kayla. That's just the way He is."

The veil of judgmental blindness lifts. I see Jared for who he really is, not perfect by any means. One of God's works in progress.

I don't know what comes over me. Before I know it, I'm telling him my darkest secret. Twisting a tissue into knots, I begin. "I loved someone once." I turn to see his reaction. He doesn't take his eyes off the road, but I know he hears me because he swallows hard. "I gave him everything and then he moved on to someone else. I've never forgiven myself for being so stupid and gullible."

Stillness separates us. I'm certain Jared is shocked by my confession. My heart presses against my rib cage as I await his judgment. He glances sideways and nods. "I figured it was something like that." On another breath he adds, "I'm not perfect, Kayla. You of all people should know that. I'm not proud of my past, but I'm ready to settle down with one woman and I'd like that woman to be you."

By now the tissue is in shreds in my lap. My heart is hanging in the balance as I look through glassy eyes. "Even with all my hang-ups?"

He reaches across the seat and takes my hand. Tiny lines frame his eyes. His lips turn up into a smile. "Yes."

Only a few days ago I was certain Jared and I had no future. I'm still not certain we do, but I'm willing to explore the possibility. Returning his smile, I say, "Can we be friends first and see where that leads us?"

Jared exhales and laughs. "Okay, friends first, but don't keep me waiting too long."

The meaning behind his words shocks me. When I gain control, I remind him we are on our way to church, and he reminds me God created male and female.

We arrive and find the parking lot full so Jared parks on the street. Quickly, because we are late, he gets out of the vehicle and comes around to open my door. When I step out onto the sidewalk, a brisk wind whirls around my nylon covered legs. I shiver in the icy coldness. Seeing this, Jared pulls me into the crook of his arm and hurries me toward the front doors of the church where a line is forming. I catch a glimpse of Derek. He's just inside the open doors, smiling and shaking hands with well wishers. He must feel my stare because he looks directly at me. In the instant our eyes meet I know he's made the right decision for his life. I've never seen him so happy. If I didn't realize it before, I do now; he was meant to be a man of God. It just took him a little while to hear the calling.

Jared squeezes my shoulder, and I look up at him.

"What are you thinking?" he asks.

I let out a sigh. "Derek is so together. He's incredible."

"Should I be worried?" There's a twinkle in his eye that says he's teasing so I ponder the question.

When I've dangled him long enough, I say, "No, Derek and I are just friends."

Jared rears back and gives me a thin smile. "Excuse me. Didn't you tell me you wanted us to begin by being friends?"

I see his play on words and jab him in the ribs with my elbow. "We have a different kind of friendship."

"Like how?" he asks, baiting me with a mischievous grin.

"You know what I mean."

Our conversation is cut short when we find ourselves in front of Derek. Derek gives us a long, hard look and then smiles. He shakes hands with Jared and then wraps me in his arms.

"I knew it was him all along," he whispers in my ear.

Quietly, so Jared doesn't hear, I reply, "How did you get so smart?"

Derek chuckles and releases me while the older ladies of the congregation wear curious smiles. In a church the size of ours, rumors of romance run rampant, especially among women with very little to occupy their time. To stop wagging tongues, he reaches for Jared and wraps an arm around his shoulder. Speaking loud and clear, he says, "I wish the two of you all the best."

My cheeks turn crimson with the insinuation we're a couple. Rather than say something, I clamp my mouth shut and let the busy bodies think what they want. Jared is more than happy to add fodder to the rumor mill. He drops a kiss on my cheek and accepts Derek's well wishes with a broad smile.

"The two of you will be staying after the service for coffee and dessert, won't you?" Derek asks before turning his attention to the couple behind us.

"Of course, wouldn't miss it," Jared says.

As we walk down the aisle toward the front and some empty seats, I scowl at Jared. Beneath my breath I say, "That wasn't funny. The two of you should be ashamed of yourselves teasing those old ladies like that."

Still looking ahead, Jared speaks from the corner of his mouth. "I wasn't teasing, my dear. And I expect Derek wasn't either. He knows we belong together."

The airport is teaming with holiday travelers so Jared and I wait by the baggage carousal for Mom and Laura. I see

Mom first then my eyes gravitate to the young woman wearing dark glasses, walking with a white cane. Laura's black hair is gathered at the nape of her neck with a ribbon. She's wearing a long, cream colored coat over brown slacks. Fashionable leather boots adorn her feet. At once I wonder if all of this is due to Mom's generosity. A sliver of jealousy creeps into my heart and I bid it to go away. Mom's eyes find mine, and she guides Laura toward us. On closer inspection, I discover Laura has flawless skin and ruby red lips.

While Mom embraces me, Jared introduces himself to our houseguest. Looking over Mom's shoulder at the two of them, I can see he doesn't share my dislike for Laura. In fact, he hasn't released her hand, and I'm annoyed with him for that.

He's making a fool of himself.

Mom steps back. She looks me up and down. I do the same to her. She looks wonderful, eyes sparkling, fresh faced, hardly a wrinkle anywhere. Then, remembering Laura, Mom draws Laura away from Jared.

"Laura, this is my daughter. Kayla, this is Laura."

My feet feel like lead. Willing them to move, I inch forward and take Laura's outstretched hand. She greets me with a friendly smile that exposes beautiful teeth. When she speaks, I am taken aback by her command of the English language.

"I feel as if I already know you. Your mother has told me so much about you." She says this with such warmth that I am ashamed of my jealousy.

"We've been looking forward to your arrival." I glance at Jared for backup.

"Yes, indeed we have," he replies.

Mom doesn't notice his droll tone or the mischievous look in his eye. Her attention is on the carousal which just now begins to turn. Within minutes, she spots her luggage. Seconds later she points to two other pieces I assume are Laura's. Mom motions for Jared to grab them so they don't take another turn around the carousal. He's quick to follow her instructions, and before I know it, we are on our way home with Mom chattering like a Magpie.

Another pang of jealousy stabs my heart when she tells us how she and Laura worked side by side to find adoptive parents for some of the kids in the orphanage. To make matters worse, Mom's eyes glow whenever she looks at Laura.

When Jared suggests we stop for an early dinner, I open my mouth to object, but Mom agrees with such enthusiasm I keep quiet.

Over dinner we learn that Laura has the equivalent of a Bachelor of Science Degree. "She wants to be a lawyer one day. Isn't that wonderful?"

Laura smiles demurely and changes the topic of conversation to my career as a veterinarian.

"It must be a very rewarding field," she says.

Jared immediately jumps into the conversation. He tells Mom about Thad's offer of employment. Mom is like a runaway freight train. She deduces that if I'm considering Thad's offer I must be staying in Montana permanently. All of this might have been true a few hours ago. Now I'm not so sure. I know it's childish and very selfish, but I don't want to share Mom with another woman who, for all I know, is an opportunist.

There I go again, Lord. Forgive my jealous nature. Please help me see Laura through your eyes.

Laura stands in the foyer and inhales the scent of pine and cedar. Unfortunately, she can't see the vaulted ceilings or the gleaming hardwood floors covered in expensive throw rugs. Jared hangs her coat in the hall closet while Mom shows her around the first floor. When we are alone, I tell him I'm having a bit of difficulty with Laura being here. He smiles and draws me against him.

"It's understandable. You're used to having your mother to yourself. Now you're being asked to share her. Things would be different if you had had a sister or brother." He grins down at me and adds, "Give her a chance, Kayla."

I don't tell him I have no choice.

"And this is the kitchen. I wish you could see it, Laura. Brandon spared no expense," Mom says.

Jared releases me. We walk into the kitchen in time to see Laura running her hand over the granite countertops. She smiles at the pleasurable feel. Jared and I stay out of the way while she familiarizes herself with the layout of the appliances. I'm amazed at how quickly she orientates herself.

"This is the refrigerator," Laura says.

"Yes," Mom replies as she puts on a teakettle. This strikes me as strange. Before Romania, Mom would have put on a pot of coffee. She must read my mind. Turning to Jared and me she says, "Would you two like coffee? I can make a pot."

Jared nods. "Thanks."

Mom fills the reservoir while Jared and I watch Laura tap her way around the kitchen. Then she smiles at us, and I wonder how she knows where we are. "On the flight your mother drew the layout of the kitchen on a piece of paper and helped me trace it with my fingertip."

It occurs to me that everything about their relationship is built on trust, very similar to our relationship with God. Laura trusted Mom enough to leave her home to come to the United States.

You have to admire her for that.

While the kettle boils and the coffee perks, Mom suggests we take Laura upstairs to her bedroom. I tell her I will stay downstairs to wait for the water to boil.

"If you don't mind," she says, flashing me a bright, toothy smile.

I force myself to smile back. "Not at all."

Jared follows them with two large suitcases in tow.

As I wait for the water to boil, Mom's laughter rings out. Then Jared laughs. All this gaiety fuels my jealousy. When I recognize my attitude for what it is, childish and wrong, I quickly ask God to change my feelings toward Laura. By the time the three of them come downstairs, the table is set with cups, saucers and a plate of sugar cookies. I'm determined to make Laura feel at home.

Chapter 18

Laura captivates the hearts of Aunt Sarah and Uncle Frank ten minutes after their arrival Thanksgiving afternoon. Rebecca is taken with her too. In fact, I don't think I've ever seen her so enraptured with an adult. Her inquisitive mind wants to know all there is to know about our houseguest. So, with childish enthusiasm, no question is too personal. Rebecca inquires about Laura's age and gets a straightforward answer, no hedging or scolding for inquiring about something most American women shun. Then Rebecca asks Laura about her family. When Laura explains she was raised in an orphanage, Rebecca's smile is replaced with such profound sadness Laura feels the change in her attitude.

"It wasn't so bad," Laura assures her. "I had plenty of kids to play with. And every so often the wealthy families in town cleaned out their closets of unwanted clothing and brought them to the orphanage, and I never went to bed hungry."

Rebecca's eyes widen. "I didn't think about food." Without pause she asks, "Did you have to sleep three to a bed?"

Laura's laughter rings out, and everyone joins in.

"Heaven's no. Each of us had a bed." Laura draws Rebecca into the fold of her arms and looks down at her. "I had many stuffed animals on my bed, gifts from the ladies of the church."

Rebecca's eyes brighten with questions. "Did you have an Elmo?"

Laura pretends to ponder the question. "I think I did—not a talking one, though." With a sigh, she adds, "My favorite toy was a bear with a leather nose and beads for eyes."

Turning to Aunt Sarah, Rebecca says, "We should clean out my toy box and give all of it to the orphanage in Romania."

Aunt Sarah beams with pride. "That's an excellent idea. If we hurry, the toys will arrive in time for Christmas."

As I watch the different expressions pass across Laura's face, I understand why Mom is so drawn to her. She doesn't allow her blindness to stand in the way of enjoying life. I'm amazed at how easily she fits in with people she just met. As if I'm the visitor, I sit back and listen to Laura explain to the others how she and Mom met. I'm so engrossed in her story I don't hear the doorbell. By the time I do hear it, the person outside is holding the bell down.

"Someone should get that," Jared says.

I bite back unkind words and smile politely. When no one makes a move to answer the door, I expel an exasperated breath and stand. The doorbell rings again, and I call out, "Hold your horses, I'm coming."

"It's cold out here," a masculine voice replies.

I open the door and drag Thad into the foyer. The icy wind that follows him sends a chill down my spine. My face must register surprise because he says, "Jared invited me or did he forget to tell you?"

I cover the lie with a smile. "Of course not, it's nice to see you have the time off." I hang his coat in the closet and take the arm Thad offers.

When we enter the den, we are the focus of attention. Uncle Frank and Jared take time out of their conversation about cattle prices to shake hands with Thad. Turns out, Uncle Frank and Thad are acquainted. Why should that surprise me? Thad's a large animal vet. Aunt Sarah greets him warmly too. Even Rebecca takes her attention away from Laura to jump off the couch and run into Thad's open arms. She kisses his cheek then pulls him toward Laura.

Rebecca beams with pride and says, "This is Laura. Aunt Maggie brought her home from Romania."

Everyone bursts into laughter and Rebecca looks around the room. "What's so funny?"

Aunt Sarah dries her eyes with the back of her hand and hugs Rebecca close. "We're laughing at you, honey, you made it sound like Laura is some sort of trophy."

Rebecca's face turns crimson.

Thad moves toward Laura with his hand outstretched. When she doesn't take it, he reaches down and picks her hand up and holds it a moment.

"It's nice to meet you, Laura."

The sound of his voice changes Laura's expression. She tilts her chin upwards and breathes in Thad's essence.

"Your hands are cold," she says and then follows that profound statement with, "Hello."

Thad makes a crack about cold hands and a warm heart. His eyes don't leave Laura's face which tells me he's fallen under her spell like the rest of them. I have the urge to snap my fingers in front of his face, but I am sidetracked when pots and pans rattle in the kitchen.

Aunt Sarah quickly stands. "I think that's my sister's way of asking for help," she says on her way out of the room.

"I'll see what I can do to help," I tell the others. When Laura makes a move to stand, I add, "Laura, make sure Jared keeps wood on the fire…please."

With a nod of her pretty head, Laura sits down. On my way out of the room I see Rebecca curl up beside Laura. Jared and Uncle Frank stand with Thad near the fireplace, warming their backsides. The sound of wood burning and carols playing on the DVD add to the festive scene. As I walk away I hear Rebecca say, "You speak good English."

Laura's laughter follows me down the hall. I stop and listen.

"I studied English as a second language," she explains to Rebecca, adding, "I always knew I'd come to America one day."

Even on this day of thanksgiving, when I should be grateful for all I have, I find myself a bit envious of Laura. To make matters worse, I arrive in the kitchen and hear Aunt Sarah singing Laura's praises. Rather than intrude, I stand in the open doorway a moment until Mom feels my presence and looks over her shoulder.

"Is Laura all right?" she asks.

I let out a breath to curb my impulse to tell her Laura is a grown woman.

"She's in good hands, don't worry."

The tone of my voice causes Aunt Sarah to seek my face. In that instant I know she understands my confusion about Laura. She smiles and hands me a dishtowel. Together we dry the pots and pans that are too big to go in the dishwasher. All the while Mom chatters about Romania and how she hopes to return next spring. This comes as a surprise to me.

She turns to us with glassy eyes. "Oh, Sarah, there are so many babies that need to be loved and cuddled. Some of them will never be adopted, and that breaks my heart."

Jared walks in. His presence ends a conversation better left for another day. He walks across the room and peeks in every pot on the stove. When he reaches for the oven door handle, Mom slaps his wrist. "No peeking until dinner." She flips her dishtowel and sends him out of the kitchen. "Go stoke the fire or something."

On his way out he winks at me. Aunt Sarah doesn't miss this small gesture of affection. She raises an eyebrow and, without a word, attempts to extract an explanation from me. I ignore her until she moves in front of me and stands there.

"What?" I say.

Mom turns around and sees the game we are playing. She wipes her hands on her apron. "What's going on with the two of you?"

Aunt Sarah shrugs. "Maybe you should ask Kayla."

Throwing up my hands, I say, "Honestly, I don't know what she's talking about."

"Oh, you don't, do you? Jared comes in here, wanders around a minute and then on his way out, winks at you, and you say there isn't anything going on. Is everyone blind but me?"

Mom is speechless. Her beautiful face goes blank as she waits for an explanation.

I let out an exasperated sigh. "We are friends, nothing more."

Aunt Sarah says, "Humph." She grins and waits while Mom begins to twitter like a nervous bird. Her words roll together, but I get the meaning. She isn't moving until I tell the truth.

"Okay, we're working on a relationship."

Mom and Aunt Sarah's eyes widen with surprise. In a flurry of motion, I'm wrapped in four arms. Like silly schoolgirls, Mom and Aunt Laura swing me back and forth until laughter bubbles out of me. It's been a long time since I laughed for the sheer joy of it and it feels good.

All the noise and laughter brings Jared back to the room. He stops in the open doorway and stares at us in confusion. I give Mom and Aunt Sarah a look that tells them not to say a word. As if I'm on fire, they release me and go back to work,

Mom stirring gravy, Aunt Sarah draining the potatoes in preparation for mashing.

"Anything I can do to help?" Jared asks as he moves further into the room.

His stomach rumbles and Mom smiles over her shoulder. "You can carve the turkey."

Jared goes to the countertop and snatches the cover off the bird. "Maggie, you've outdone yourself." He stares at the golden brown turkey with stuffing bursting out of the neck. He makes the first slice and groans with anticipation.

"No fair tasting," I tell him as I leave the kitchen with the sweet potatoes. Mom and Aunt Sarah follow with other delectable dishes and return to the kitchen. I'm alone, staring at the beautiful spread. Glassware and china sparkle beneath the crystal chandelier. I'm in my own little world when Jared comes in with the turkey, which he sets in the center of the table. He lights the candles on either side of the golden bird, and for a moment I stand in awe of Mom's ability to put on this fabulous feast without making it look difficult. Moment's later, without her apron, Mom brings Laura into the dining room followed by Aunt Sarah, Uncle Frank, Rebecca and Thad. Jared pulls out a chair for Laura, and once she is seated, he indicates the chair next to her for Thad. Jared sits at one end of the table, Uncle

Frank at the other. Mom and Aunt Sarah sit on either side of Uncle Frank, Rebecca and I sit on either side of Jared.

Mom nods to Rebecca, prearranged I expect. Rebecca's prayer is simple. She asks God's blessing on the food and the family members. She thanks Him for Laura's visit and prays for the children in the Romanian orphanage. My heart swells with pride at her eloquence. I admire her child-like faith. Following her amen the meal begins with everyone passing their plates to Jared to be filled with turkey. After that, the side dishes are passed, and I watch as Thad spoons a little bit of everything on Laura's plate.

"Potatoes at one o'clock, stuffing at three o'clock, turkey at six o'clock," he tells her.

Laura looks sideways and smiles. "I see you've been around blind people before."

"My grandfather was blind," he replies.

I'm in awe of God's provisions. Long before Mom asked Laura to return to Montana, God sent Thad to this part of the country to offer me a job in the veterinary clinic and help Laura adjust to Montana. As if he reads my mind, Thad looks up from his meal and smiles at me. "So, have you given any thought to the job offer?"

Everyone quietly awaits my answer.

"Yes, I have. I've decided to accept the position."

"That's great. It will be wonderful having you aboard."

"Oh, Kayla," Mom gushes.

I shake my head and Mom bites back further comment. I can tell by the hurt expression on her face that she feels left out of my decision.

"We'll talk later, okay?" I tell her.

Mom nods and manages a small smile I return. Then, with a sigh, I turn to Jared. He gives me a playful grin that tugs at my heart. But I remind myself the sexual attraction between us isn't enough. I hope he doesn't take this decision to mean I've decided the course of the rest of my life, because I haven't. I have, however, come to realize making choices on my own, without God's blessing, only leads to unhappiness. So, if Jared is to be my life-long partner, then God will have to convince me.

That evening, after the house is quiet, I knock on Laura's bedroom door. She calls for me to come in. I peek around the open door and see that she is in bed. Laura looks lovely in light pink pajamas, propped up against the headboard with several pillows. As I draw near, I notice the Braille Bible lying open in her lap.

I swallow hard and speak before losing my confidence.

"Laura, I'd like to explain something to you."

She draws a breath and lets it out. Then she waits for me to continue.

"I was prepared not to like you. Does that surprise you?"

With a shake of her head, she replies, "No, I suspected as much."

Her eyes well up with tears as she reaches into space and waits for me to take her hand. "When your mother invited me to come to America, I asked her how you would feel. She said you wouldn't mind, but I tried on your shoes and asked myself how I would feel."

I laugh at her translation of this well known phrase.

"Am I not saying it right?" she asks.

"You're doing just fine," I reply, squeezing her hand.

Laura's face brightens. It's easy to see my acceptance of her is what she has been longing for.

Out of curiosity I say, "If you were worried about what I would think, why did you take Mom up on the offer?"

Laura bites her lip and struggles with her emotions. "It is important that I see again so I can return to my country to work for reform in the orphanages so that the children will have a better life."

Her unselfish attitude does me in. I ask myself if I would have the courage to leave my country and move to a foreign land. Within the space of a few minutes my opinion of Laura changes. I take her in my arms. She rests her head on my shoulder, and I feel her small body shudder.

"We will do all we can to help," I whisper into her hair.

Chapter 19

There are days I find myself envious of Laura. She personifies the word grace and fills the void Brandon's death left in my mother's heart. Laura gives Mom purpose. Even so, it doesn't make it any easier to watch them together. They share a common dream to return to the orphanage where Laura grew up. I remind myself Laura is blind and the reason she is here in the first place is to regain her sight. Mom is confident that will happen, so is Doctor Culbreath, the young and very talented surgeon who will operate on Laura's eyes the week after Christmas. Having Laura here is doing me some good, too. She is teaching me the true meaning of humility, a quality I lack and one so necessary if I am to follow the example of Jesus. I shouldn't be, but I am amazed at God's wisdom through all of this. After all, He is the creator of the universe, so bringing a blind woman and a hurting family together is a small job for Him. Even Jared responds to Laura. His face lights up when she enters the room. The two of them spend hours sitting in front of the fire discussing their favorite authors. What bugs me is that Laura has only been here a short while and she knows Jared better than I do.

It's the week before Christmas. With a reluctant groan, I open my eyes and turn my head. The first light of dawn rises over the distant hills, a perfect backdrop for the snow flurries drifting past my bedroom window. The night before the weatherman on the local television channel spoke of below zero temperatures for today. The thought of driving to the clinic on the icy back roads causes my stomach to tighten. Silly, I know, but I've never gotten over the accident I had many years ago; blackout conditions, icy, winding road and a snowplow that came out of nowhere. My life changed from that point on. The dreams I had of winning a world championship in women's barrel racing were shattered as I hung upside down in the twisted remains of my automobile.

I push the frightening scene from my mind and toss aside the covers. In the bathroom, I brush my teeth and pull my wayward tresses into a pony tail, which I secure with an elastic band. Knowing how drafty and cold the clinic is, I dress in layers of insulated underwear, blue jeans, t-shirt, sweater, heavy socks and boots. A quick glance in the mirror tells me I look heavier than my usual one-hundred twenty-seven pounds.

Oh, well, the animals won't notice. They don't care how I look anyway.

On my way downstairs, I meet Jared in the foyer. His jacket is covered in a light dusting of snow.

"Good morning, bright eyes," he says and turns to hang his jacket in the hall closet.

Jared is wearing Wranglers and a red and grey plaid flannel shirt with a hint of white t-shirt showing at the neck. He leaves his winter boots in the closet and stuffs his feet in fur-lined slippers. His dark hair is plastered to his head thanks to a knitted snow cap Mom made. Before turning around, he tucks his gloves into the pocket of his jacket and tells me he's been out in the pastures checking the cattle.

"Thank God for snowmobiles. A man riding a horse would still be out there," he says, dropping an arm around my shoulder. He gives me a peck on the cheek, and we stroll into the kitchen together.

Other than these little displays of affection, Jared is respecting my decision to take our relationship one day at a time. I must say he's not the same Jared I knew before I left Montana to attend college. He's as attractive as ever, but there's something different about him; he has mellowed over the past ten years.

Mom glances at us from behind the morning newspaper. "Coffee's ready and there's scrambled eggs and bacon on the stove." She does her best to hide her smile of approval behind a look of nonchalance.

I follow Jared to the coffee pot, watch him pour two cups, add cream and hand me one. Our eyes meet until the tap of Laura's cane against the hardwood flooring in the hallway interrupts the moment. Jared sets his cup down on the counter and hurries to greet our houseguest as she enters the kitchen. Mom lays the newspaper aside and joins Jared and Laura.

"You look lovely, doesn't she Jared?" Mom says, taking Laura's arm.

Jared gives Laura an admiring glance and says, "That she does. Blue suits you, Laura."

He is referring to the light blue, long-sleeved sweater that compliments Laura's milky complexion. She cocks her head and smiles up at him.

"Thank you. Men in my country wouldn't notice."

Jared is about to open his mouth when I jump into the conversation. "Good morning, Laura, how did you sleep?" I ask as I lean against the kitchen counter sipping coffee.

She turns in the direction of my voice. "Like a tree."

Mom erupts into laughter. "No, no, dear, not like a tree. You slept like a log."

Laura's cheeks turn a delicate pink. "Yes, a log." She lets out a frustrated sigh. "I don't think I will ever understand the English language. There are so many strange phrases."

The room fills with laughter. I must admit it feels good this early in the morning.

Jared steals Laura from Mom and leads her to the table, though I daresay she doesn't need any help finding it. "How about some breakfast?" he asks on his way to the cupboard where he retrieves two plates. He looks over his shoulder at me and then Laura.

"Yes, please," Laura says while unfolding a napkin in her lap.

"And you?" Jared asks, turning to me.

"Yes, please."

I sit across from Laura. Mom takes her place and picks up the newspaper. She speaks from behind it. "I think we're in for a good storm. Honey, you be careful driving to the clinic."

Jared sets a plate of food in front of Laura. Her silverware has been arranged so she knows where knife, fork and spoon are. Her cup of coffee and juice is strategically arranged too. Jared returns to the table carrying two plates, one for me and one for Laura. In the morning light, the gray around his temples is more prominent. Tiny lines frame his eyes. He smiles at me and bows his head and I see Brandon in him. The thought of Brandon makes my heart ache. For a moment I wish I had opted to go to college in Montana. Then I remind myself that hindsight doesn't serve good purpose.

Table talk centers on the weather, Lady's pregnancy and her due date, which is rapidly approaching. If she is on time, we'll have a frisky foal in the barn by the end of January. I'm looking forward to this blessed event since I missed the birth of her other babies while I was away at college and completing my internship.

The grandfather clock in the hallway strikes seven. Quickly, because I know it will take twice as long to drive to work, I clear my dishes, bid farewell to Mom and Laura and head for the coat closet with Jared on my heels. He helps me into my coat, buttons it up to my chin and places a knitted stocking cap on my head. Opening the door, he brushes my cheek with a kiss and sends me off.

"I'll drop by later and take you to lunch. Call me if an emergency arises and you can't make it."

My cheeks feel numb as I run around the side of the house, to the garage. I enter through the side door, press the automatic door opener and climb into the Suburban. As I drive past the house, Mom is standing at the window, curtain drawn. She waves and the curtain flutters back into place. I drive slowly down the driveway and stop for a doe and fawn as they trot past the front of the Suburban and disappear into a dense growth of pines. Rabbits scurry across the pristine whiteness, leaving paw prints in their wake. Bright red Cardinals sitting amongst the snow covered branches, a sight that takes my breath away.

J. B. Williams

Chapter 20

It is my good fortune to follow the snowplow to the clinic. Dana, the veterinary technician and sometime receptionist, meets me at the door. She is breathless. "Thank God you're here. Thad is home with the flu and there's an emergency at the Brown Ranch. One of the older horses slipped and fell. Clarence thinks the old girl broke her leg. She's down, and she won't get up."

"I'm on it." I grab the keys to the veterinary truck on the way out.

I'm halfway to the truck when I remember that I didn't ask Dana if there were any patients in the waiting room that needed my services. *If there are, they'll have to wait.* I slide into the cab of the truck, stick the key in the ignition and listen to the motor cough and sputter and finally come to life. The

Brown Ranch is several miles away. As I drive, I think about the old mare on the cold ground. Clarence Brown is eighty with white hair and blue eyes that look at a person as if he knows something they don't. When I get out of the truck, Clarence meets me. There's no twinkle in his eyes today.

"She's around back." He motions with a wave of his gnarled hand, and I trudge after him through knee deep snow.

The old mare is a hundred-fifty feet from the back of the barn, laying there like she hasn't got a care in the world. Beneath her is a thick layer of ice covering the creek.

"Guess she decided to go skating," I say in an attempt to lighten what I'm thinking is going to be a very sad event.

Clarence glances sideways at me and puffs out a breath of air. It hangs in front of him. He doesn't find me funny. As we draw near, I see that her leg is in an odd position. The mare groans in pain as I drop to my knees. When I try to examine the leg, she flattens her ears against her head and tries to bite me.

I glance up at the rancher. "How old is she, Clarence?"

Clarence ponders my question with raised brow. "Guess she's thirty, maybe thirty-one."

With a sigh, I stand and brush the snow off my jeans. This gives me time to make up my mind how to phrase my next statement. I turn my back on my patient and lower my voice.

"We need to put her down, Clarence. There's no way

she'll make it through surgery let alone a couple months hanging in a sling to keep the weight off the leg."

Clarence doesn't speak. He just stares down at his horse through teary eyes. He knows there isn't, but he asks anyway.

"Isn't there another choice?"

I shake my head and wait until Clarence nods.

Together we trudge back to the truck. Clarence watches me fill three syringes. I grab a couple of horse cookies and we go back to the mare. Her eyes tell me she's in a lot of pain. Holding out my hand, I offer her a treat but she ignores it—kind of like she's saying, get on with it.

Clarence kneels and cradles her head in his lap. I find the vein right off. The old mare doesn't flinch when I pierce the skin. The first syringe puts her to sleep within a few seconds. I remove the first syringe from the needle and attach the second which I slowly empty into the vein. I remove that one from the needle and attach the third. When it's empty, I check for a heartbeat.

"She's gone, Clarence," I say.

The old man nods and slips from beneath the heavy head. The old mare's eyes are dull and lifeless. Clarence tries to pull the eyelids down, but they refuse to stay shut.

While he goes to get a blanket to cover the mare, I place my hand on her side and whisper, "Go to the light, old girl."

Tears spill down my cheeks. I guess I'll never get used to this part of my job. Countless times I've told myself that once an animal loses dignity, it's time to let go. But, nevertheless, it's hard to do what has to be done.

Boots crunching through the snow alert me that Clarence is coming back. Before he catches me crying, I draw a gloved hand across my eyes. Together we spread an old horse blanket over the mare. Clarence and I walk back to the truck. He waits while I write out a bill. This is another area of veterinary medicine I dislike—giving someone a bill for putting their animal to sleep; it doesn't seem right somehow.

Clarence hands me five twenty dollar bills. I give him a receipt and tell him I'll call the rendering plant to request they send a truck out to pick up the mare. He nods and sniffs back tears. Quickly, so he doesn't break down in front of me, I climb in the truck and drive off. Clarence is from a generation of men who don't show their emotions, especially not in front of a woman and certainly not about an old ranch horse.

When I arrive at the clinic, Dana hands me another call sheet. And this is the way my morning goes. By twelve-thirty I'm famished. Jared's truck is parked in front of the clinic when I pull up. He's sitting in the waiting room reading a cattle magazine. My voice brings a smile to his face. He sets the magazine aside and stands and comes toward me. I must look a sight because he brushes stray strands of hair that have escaped the pony tail behind my ear and kisses my cheek. I hear Dana sigh and peer over Jared's shoulder at her. Her face turns red with embarrassment, and she quickly finds filing to do.

"I'm famished," I announce.

I don't know how he arranged it, but I don't have another appointment until two-thirty—plenty of time to get something to eat. Jared grins and takes my elbow. We're out the door and in his truck before I have time to get cold. He glances sideways as he turns the key in the ignition. "What do you feel like…Mexican, Chinese, or a good old greasy hamburger?"

"I think I'll clog my arteries."

"McDonalds it is then."

Half the teenagers in town are here. So is Nathan, but that isn't surprising. He's probably keeping an eye on his football team. He acknowledges us with a smile. Jared nods and I wave back. I heard through the grapevine that Nathan and his girlfriend set a date. Good for them.

Jared and I order double cheeseburgers, fries and Cokes. I've always found it kind of senseless to eat a meal like this and order Diet Coke, but I do it anyway.

We take our order to an out-of-the-way table where Jared asks about my morning.

"I put Clarence Brown's old mare down first thing. It snowballed from there. Next stop the Thompson Ranch. Seems their stallion decided to run through the barb wire fence."

Jared swallows and says, "Not their good cutting horse!"

"None other. Good thing he isn't in the halter division because he's got a six inch gash across his chest. It took thirty stitches to close the wound."

My cell phone rings. I answer and Dana tells me my afternoon appointment cancelled. Jared raises an eyebrow.

"Don't ask me," I say, "Maybe they decided the goat wasn't worth a vet call and took matters into their own hands."

On the way back to the clinic, Jared asks me if we are any closer to announcing our engagement. I glance sideways and give him an amused smile. "How romantic, just what a girl will remember when she's sitting on the porch in her rocking chair."

"I tried the romance thing, remember? So, are you any closer to making up your mind?"

The truck stops in front of the clinic. Without answering him, I open the door and jump out. I figure he's coming after me, but when I get to the clinic door he's sitting in the truck. With some reluctance, I walk to his side of the truck. He rolls down the window. There's a shadow of hurt in his eyes.

"Can we talk about this later?" I ask.

"We don't have to talk about it at all, if you don't want," he says and puts the truck in reverse.

I stare after him as he drives away. For the rest of the day I kick myself for being so stubborn. In my heart I know that I want to spend the rest of my life with him.

Then why am I having so much trouble committing to him?

The rest of my day is spent looking after in-house patients, all of them post surgery. It's hard to imagine, but I removed two baby diapers from a pet goat's stomach. Seems he tipped over the garbage can and devoured everything chewable inside. The absorbent material in the baby diapers soaks up hundreds of times its weight, and since the goat couldn't pass the diaper through his intestines, he was dehydrated. My other two patients, elderly horses, are recovering from colic surgery.

By the time six o'clock rolls around, I'm exhausted. I stop by the reception desk, and Dana informs me Thad is no better, which means I will be on call tonight. I give her a tired smile and reach for my jacket and knitted cap. On the way out, I call over my shoulder. "I'm taking the vet truck home just in case I have an overnight emergency."

"Okay, let's hope it's a quiet night," Dana calls after me.

It's snowing, big fluffy snowflakes. I tilt my head back and catch one on my tongue. As I drive home, I rehearse what to say to Jared.

"Sorry about this afternoon. You caught me off guard."

My words sound hollow and echo in the cold cab.

"Yes, I've given our relationship a lot of thought lately. I agree it's time to move ahead."

The thought of marriage and being responsible to another human being sends a wave of panic over me.

"Cut it out. You're acting like an immature kid," I tell myself as I look in the rearview mirror. "I'll wait until we're alone and tell him I'll marry him in the spring."

Before I know it, I'm turning into the gates of McChesney Ranch. I park the veterinary truck in the garage and enter the house through the kitchen. The aroma of roast beef greets me. I hang my jacket on the peg by the back door and stuff my knitted cap and gloves into a pocket. Mom is no where to be found, so I head toward the voices in the den. I find Jared and Laura sitting on the sofa. There's an old photo album in his lap. Unaware of my presence, he describes each picture. One in particular brings about a round of laughter.

"What's so funny?" I ask upon entering the room.

Laura's face blooms into a wide smile. "Hi, Kayla, Jared is showing me family pictures. How was your day?"

I flop into an arm chair and expel a breath. "Nothing out of the ordinary—just another day. How was yours?"

"Good. I helped Maggie make cookies."

"Speaking of Mom, where is she? She wasn't in the kitchen when I came home."

Jared answers. "She went over to Sarah's for the afternoon. There's a roast in the oven. Maggie said she'll be home in time to take it out."

His eyes linger on me a moment and then he returns his attention to the photo album. "This one is of Dad when he was about three, maybe four. He's butt naked, wearing grandpa's work boots and an old cowboy hat."

Laura chuckles at the vivid picture Jared paints with words. He smiles at me and I push my aching body out of the chair. "Since I have time, I'm going upstairs to take a bath."

"Good idea," he says.

I climb the staircase to my bedroom and gather fresh clothing. The shared bathroom down the hall contains an old-fashioned bathtub with clawed legs and a slanted back meant for relaxing. I turn on the taps and add a heaping tablespoon of bath salts to the cascading water. The room fills with steam as I drop my clothing to the floor. With a groan of pleasure, I lower myself into the tub and close my eyes. My next recollection is a knock on the door. As my mind clears, I realize the water is tepid, nearly cold.

A glance at my watch stirs me to action.

"Kayla, are you in there?"

"Yes, Mother, I'll be right out."

"Dinner is ready. It's getting cold."

"I'll hurry. Go ahead and start without me."

When I walk into the dining room, Jared stands and pulls out my chair. He brushes his lips across my cheek and murmurs, "You look nice—smell nice, too."

I ignore the hidden meaning in his remark and sit down. While I fix a plate, Mother inquires about my day. When I tell her I had to put the old mare down, she sympathizes with Clarence.

"I'll take a pie over to them and see how they're doing."

"That would be nice," I say and bow my head to say grace.

The roast beef melts in my mouth, along with the oven roasted potatoes. When I finish eating, I lean back in my chair and groan with delight.

"I hope you saved some room for cookies," Mom says while pushing herself away from the table.

She disappears out the door and returns with a plate of chocolate chip cookies and a carafe of coffee. Not long after the last cookie is eaten, Mom, with Laura's help, clears the table. When I arise to help, Mom says, "Sit down and relax. Laura and I are capable of loading the dishwasher."

On her way out of the room, Mom glances over her shoulder and smiles at Jared. My gut tells me the two of them are up to something. I don't have to wait long to find out what it is. When we are alone, Jared reaches for my hand. "I'm sorry about this afternoon. I acted like a complete idiot."

His apology takes me by surprise.

"No, you have every right to expect an answer to your proposal. You've been very patient with me."

The room goes quiet. Uncertainty fills Jared's eyes.

In a shaky voice I say, "I love you, Jared. I'm not sure what kind of wife I will be, but if you are willing to have me as I am, then the answer is yes."

Jared is out of his chair and I'm in his arms. His kiss is soft and tender. He nibbles on my bottom lip while staring into my eyes and my senses take off like a bottle rocket.

"Is spring soon enough?" I ask.

I feel his heart beat against my chest. In a raspy voice he says, "I was thinking more on the lines of January 1st. What a great way to start the New Year."

Rearing back in his arms, I study him for sincerity. "You're not kidding, are you?"

"No, I'm not."

"But weddings take time…"

His kiss cuts me off mid-sentence. When our lips part, he says, "Not if we turn Maggie loose." There's a twinkle in his eye. "January 1st and we'll honeymoon in Mexico."

Chapter 21

Anyone else would crumble under such pressure, but Mom handles Christmas and wedding preparations with ease. Jared and I will be married in the living room with close friends and family in attendance, the same as Mom and Brandon many years ago. In fact, I will wear her wedding gown. Handwritten invitations will go out immediately. I'm hopeful Bryan and Clara will be here for the holidays and that they can arrange to stay longer, so she can be my matron of honor. I can't wait to see them.

Then there's the added responsibility of Laura's surgery, which has now been put off until the third week in January, a concession suggested by her so Jared and I can honeymoon in Mexico and return in time to be here when the operation takes place. All things considered, I'm holding up rather well. The clinic is busier than usual which keeps my mind off the wedding. I barely have time to shop for Christmas gifts. Then, surprise of surprises, Rebecca, my niece calls. She needs help searching for just the right gift for Aunt Sarah and Uncle Frank, so I arrange to pick her up on Wednesday, my day off.

Jared seems oblivious to the crunch of time. He goes about his daily routine. The only difference—he smiles a lot. If we meet in the hall, he stops to kiss me. It seems he finds any excuse to kiss me now that the wedding date is set.

December 15th, 2:30 a.m. My beeper rings. Thad beckons me to join him on a serious call. A cow expelled her uterus while giving birth. I stagger of bed and pull on long underwear, jeans, and stuff my feet into warm socks and then into boots. I layer t-shirt, sweatshirt and a wool shirt on my upper torso and slip from my room. To my surprise, Jared meets me in the hall, dressed and ready to go.

"I'm going with you." He gives me a look that says *no argument.*

We exit the house and run to the garage. The Suburban fires up about the same time the garage door opens. He drives according to my directions, and we stop in front of the calving barn at the Robertson Ranch. Thad is with the cow. She's lying in a bed of straw with a healthy calf standing beside her. Blood surrounds the uterus, which has already been washed and is lying on a plastic tarp.

Thad glances up at me. "We'll give her an epidural. Can you fill a syringe?"

Jared follows me and backs the truck into the center of the barn.

I hand him a pair of palpation gloves. "Put these on. We might need your help."

After filling the syringe, I put on a pair of gloves and hurry back to the calving area. Thad administers the epidural while the cow lays there chewing her cud, a contented look on her face. Once the epidural takes effect, Thad encourages the cow to get up. As she rises, Jared and Phil Robertson take hold of the four corners of the tarp and lift. The tarp now becomes our work table in the absence of a real one. Thad and I begin to stuff the uterus into the cow's vagina. Sweat beads on our brows as we struggle with the massive mound of tissue and muscle. It's rough going for a while, but once we get it halfway in, it seems to remember where it belongs. But, before we are finished, the epidural begins to lose its anesthetic ability. The cow squirms and threatens to kick. Phil Robertson goes to her head and squeezes her nose with his fingers. Jared lifts her tail and bends it back. All this takes her mind off what's happening.

She settles down and Thad does a final examination and positions her womb.

"That should do it," he says, withdrawing his arm from inside the cow. He turns skeptical eyes on Phil. "She might expel the uterus again if she strains too hard. Keep her quiet and away from the other cows for a couple weeks." Thad pulls off his gloves and tosses them in the waste receptacle in the back of his vet truck. Jared and I do the same.

Jared shakes hands with his fellow rancher while Thad and I confer on follow-up procedure. "On your way in to work tomorrow, stop by and take the cow's temperature. I'll leave antibiotics for Phil to administer to her," Thad says.

He goes back for another look at the cow now standing quietly with her nursing calf. Once assured she is okay, at least for the moment, he joins Jared and me near the Suburban.

"Thanks, I couldn't have done that without your help." Thad gives us a tired smile and adds, "Might as well get used to late night calls, Jared. That's the norm when you marry a vet."

Jared chuckles and helps me into the Suburban. Before closing the door, he leans in to kiss me. Like I said, he shows a lot more affection as of late.

On the way home, he tells me how proud he is of me. "Most women wouldn't be able to do what you do."

I give him a tired smile of gratitude and rest my head against the back of the seat. Upon our arrival home, we go upstairs. Jared holds me close, and even though I smell foul, he plants tiny kisses all over my face; then his demeanor changes. His God-given sexual drive kicks in. His arms tighten and for a minute I lose myself in his embrace. His need and my need come together with such urgency it takes all my self-control to push him away.

Through gasps of breath I plead with him to help me remain loyal to our pledge to wait until our wedding night. This plea puts the burden on him and lets him know how much I love and want to be with him. He nods and reaches behind me to open my bedroom door. Gently, Jared pushes me inside and closes the door behind me.

All my clothing goes in the hamper. I wash my hands and arms up to my elbows and brush my teeth. Once I'm in bed I thank God for the wonderful, caring individual Jared has become and I ask Him to give me what it takes to be a good wife.

The following morning my eyes pop open at the sound of my bedroom door opening. Jared comes in with a breakfast tray. "Good morning, sleepy head. It's seven-thirty," he says, entering the room.

"What's this?" I ask, pushing myself into a sitting position.

Jared sets the tray in front of me and grins. "Breakfast, eat it before it gets cold. And, remember, you're taking Rebecca Christmas shopping today."

That reminder triggers another appointment, this one with a lady from the church who is dropping by around nine o'clock to fit my wedding dress. Mom was skin and bones when she married Brandon, so seams will have to be let out. I inhale the maple syrup drooling over the pancakes and groan with pleasure. Tiny link sausages are arranged alongside the stack. A tall glass of orange juice and a cup of coffee complete Jared's handiwork.

He bends down and kisses my forehead. On his way out of the room, he tells me he is off to the jewelers to pick up the rings which have been kept a secret from me until now. I feign disinterest even though I'm absolutely positive the rings are family heirlooms—most likely his grandparents' wedding bands sized to fit our fingers. His excitement is infectious. Butterflies dance in my stomach at the thought of wearing my mother's wedding dress and his grandmother's wedding ring.

The door closes and I attack the pancakes and sausage like I haven't eaten for a month. Then I take a shower and go downstairs. Mom acknowledges the empty tray with a glowing smile. Laura says, "Good morning. I hear you had an emergency last night."

While rinsing the dishes I give Mom and Laura the gory details. Laura's face turns a dingy shade of gray when I tell her we stuffed the uterus back in the cow. Mom can't help but chuckle. She's seen her share of calving problems. Setting her newspaper aside, she says, "I laid out the wedding dress. It's in the living room. As soon as the alterations are done, I've asked Mrs. Cummings to drop it off at the cleaners. We don't wear the same size, so you'll need to find a pair of shoes."

"I'll do that today, while Rebecca and I are shopping."

After loading the dishes, I go to the living room and stop in the doorway. Mom's wedding dress is spread over the back of the couch. My eyes are transfixed on the silky material when someone stirs behind me. Hands rest on my shoulders and I glance at the perfectly manicured nails.

"It's really happening, isn't it?" I say.

"Yes, it is. My little girl is getting married. By the way, your father and Joyce are coming. Did I tell you?"

"Twice, maybe three times." I glance back at her. "You really like Joyce, don't you?"

Mom's face creases into a warm smile. "Yes, I do. Your father is very lucky to have her. They are perfect together, like Brandon and I were." Her voice breaks as she speaks Brandon's name, and I know for certain that Mom will never remarry. Brandon was her first and only love. To have that kind of commitment for another human being humbles me beyond words, and I pray God grants me that kind of love for Jared.

The doorbell rings at nine o'clock. Mrs. Cummings is a plump woman with a ready smile. Her dark hair is sprinkled with gray. Gold rimmed glasses hang from a chain around her neck. She greets me with a hug and shows herself into the living room, where she takes off her jacket and drapes it over the back of an arm chair. Out of the pocket she retrieves a plastic tin of straight pins and a tape measure. The other pocket holds a pair of small sewing scissors in a fancy case and a seam ripping tool. She shuts the door and asks me to slip out of my clothes and into the dress.

I'm surprised to find it fits everywhere except the waist, which needs to be let out as much as possible. Even then I will have to starve myself to fit comfortably into the waistline. While the alterations are underway, Mom comes in and stops. Her hand goes to her mouth. Tears brighten her eyes. Laura stands behind her, eager to hear about the dress.

"She looks beautiful, Laura, like an angel." Mom draws Laura into the room and makes sure she is comfortable in the chair before joining us.

A picture is taken for posterity. Then Mom hangs the dress inside a garment bag and offers Mrs. Cummings tea. "Sorry, Maggie, I can't stay. I have Christmas shopping to do and a wedding dress to alter."

Mrs. Cummings slips into her coat and returns her alteration kit to her pocket. Before leaving, she turns in the open doorway. "Don't worry, Kayla, your dress will be done in plenty of time for the wedding," she tells me and waddles down the recently shoveled sidewalk.

I wait until her car motor turns over and then close the door. A check of my watch spurs me into action. I high-tail it to the hall closet to retrieve a jacket and gloves, exchange my tennis shoes for fur-lined boots, and after a quick goodbye to Mom and Laura, I leave through the front door. A brisk wind blows, so I hurry around the side of the house to the garage.

Uncle Frank and Aunt Sarah, with Rebecca close on their heels, greet me at the front door. Uncle Frank looks the same. His wardrobe never changes—Lee overalls over a plaid flannel shirt. Aunt Sarah's hair has a bit more gray and she's a few pounds heavier but still pretty. Rebecca stops me cold. She's as tall as I am with long, chestnut colored hair and hazel eyes.

I exchange hugs with my aunt and uncle then turn my attention to Rebecca. "Are you ready to go, kid?"

Rebecca doesn't need a second invitation. She retrieves her coat and we're out the door. White breath floats out in front of me when I ask her if she has any particular gifts in mind.

"No, that's what I need you for." Rebecca slides into the front seat of the Suburban and waits for me to get in. As soon as I pull the door closed, she grills me about our wedding plans.

"Just a small wedding, I'm afraid. Jared and I don't want to make a big deal out of it." I turn and smile at my grown-up shopping partner. "So, we have a lot of catching up to do. How about stopping for lunch? Would you like that?"

Rebecca's squirms in her seat. "Yes, please. Can we have Chinese? Mom and Dad hate Chinese, so I don't get to have it very often—only when Maggie comes and takes me out."

"Chinese it is. I know the perfect place. It's a hole in the wall, but they have the best fried rice and sweet and sour pork."

As I drive, I realize how much time I've missed with Rebecca. When I left for college she was a toddler. Now she's a blossoming pre-teen.

Conversation lapses into a comfortable silence as the landscape speeds by. Out of the corner of my eye, I see Rebecca deep in thought.

"Do you have a boyfriend?"

She makes a distasteful face. "Yuck. No."

"Methinks you protest too much."

Rebecca's cheeks turn crimson—a family trait she didn't escape.

I wink at her and press for details.

"Well, he's kind of cute," she admits of a boy in her American History class.

Taking my eyes off the road for a moment, I tease her with a smile. "Cute is okay, but nice is even better. Does he come from good family?"

Color creeps into Rebecca's cheeks again. "Gee, Kayla, I'm not going to marry him. I just said he was kind of cute. So, what's the big deal?"

I'm beginning to press my luck, so I change the subject. "Hey, kiddo, would you like to be in my wedding?"

Rebecca's face lights up and she turns in her seat. "You mean it? Honest?"

"I was thinking you might like to be my bridesmaid. I'll even splurge and buy the dress and shoes."

"For real?"

I glance sideways. Rebecca's smile exposes braces.

"Absolutely."

Chapter 22

We shop until our stomachs growl in protest. Then, rather than brave the weather outside, which has turned ugly according to another shopper, we make our way to the food court where I scan the sea of heads in search of a table. Fortunate for us, the table I find is next to one occupied by two young women with babies in booster chairs. The women look at the packages we are carrying and give us sympathetic smiles, which affords me an opportunity to ask if they'd mind keeping an eye on our shopping bags while we get something to eat.

They echo, "We'd be happy too."

"Thanks so much," I call over my shoulder as Rebecca and I weave our way through the tables to the Chinese food counter.

We order sweet and sour pork, fried rice, beef and broccoli. A glass of milk for her and a cup of tea for me complete our meals. When we return to our table, I thank the two ladies again.

"No problem," one of them says while laying her crying baby in the stroller.

I've never heard such a sound come from something so small. To make matters worse, the other baby begins to cry. The anxious mothers look around to see if anyone is staring. When they see they are the center of attention, they exit the area in a hurry. Long after they blend into the crowd, the crying babies can be heard.

Rebecca stares after the two women and sighs. "I'm never going to have kids."

I raise an amused brow. "Of course you are. Why would you say something like that?

"Because I don't want children—I'm not even sure I want to get married."

This surprises me. If Rebecca came from a broken home I might understand, but Aunt Sarah and Uncle Frank have a wonderful marriage.

"When the right man comes along, he'll sweep you off your feet and you'll change your mind."

"Is that what happened to you? Did Jared sweep you off your feet?"

Rebecca's hazel eyes probe mine.

I reach for my napkin and dab at the corners of my mouth while formulating my answer. "Jared and I were friends. When our friendship grew into something more, we decided to spend our lives together."

"But do you love him?" Rebecca leans forward and waits.

Long seconds pass. *Do I love him?*

"Yes, I love him. Now eat your lunch, Missy. I have to get you home."

Rebecca continues to watch me. I ignore her and concentrate on the plate of food in front of me. After a couple minutes I look up, and she's scowling at me.

"What?" I ask.

"You're eating too fast."

Her admonition slows me down. It also gives us time to talk.

"All we have left to do is shop for your parents," I say.

"The hardest of all," she wails. "They have everything or at least that's what Mom says." Rebecca rolls her eyes in mock disbelief. "If I had a lot of money, I'd send them on a cruise or something. They never get away from the farm."

I ponder this unselfish comment. "Maybe they don't want to get away. Maybe they are content where God has them. Ever think of it that way?"

Rebecca gives me a confused smile. "Are you saying God doesn't want them to have a vacation?"

She has me there. "You know I haven't given much thought to God's opinion of vacations, but I'm sure he doesn't mind them. Even Jesus needed a rest once in a while." Rebecca pops another piece of pork in her mouth. Then an idea comes to me. "Since you can't give them a cruise, why not give them a travel video for Christmas. Pick a place you'd like to send them."

Rebecca's face explodes into an enormous smile. The neon lights accentuate the splash of freckles across the bridge of her nose. I recall having freckles when I was her age, and I hated them. Now, looking at them through adult eyes, I see their beauty, the innocence they bring to a young face so full of life, not yet encumbered with the twists of fate that years of living bring—no, not fate. According to scripture nothing happens to us by coincidence. God is in control. My heart swells with the knowledge my life is designed by the creator of the universe.

"I love the idea," Rebecca wails. "I can send them to Israel this year. Next year I can send them to Rome. Thanks, Kayla. You're the best."

We find the perfect video at a Bible book store. When I drop her off at home, Rebecca shows off the full-length, dusty rose dress with full skirt and matching shoes. She holds it up against her body and dances around the living room. Uncle Frank whistles. Aunt Sarah's eyes shine. Their little girl is growing up.

I leave them with hugs all around and arrive home at a little before five. Jared's truck is parked in front of the house. Before I have time to press the automatic garage door opener, which is clipped to the sun visor, the door opens. I pull the Suburban in and Jared enters through the side door to help carry the packages inside.

"I was getting a tad worried," he says as I hand him two large bags containing gifts for Mom and Laura and shoes to go with my wedding dress. The bag with his gift I carry myself because he's curious by nature, and I'm afraid he will spoil my surprise.

I accept his peck on the cheek as we trudge through the snow to the back door. Inside I'm greeted by a warm kitchen and dinner, which is sitting on the stove.

"Maggie and Laura went to a concert given by the high school seniors," Jared explains with a nod toward the kitchen table where a setting for two awaits us.

Soft music comes from the stereo in the living room.

He takes the packages upstairs while I hang my jacket on the peg by the back door. Upon his return, he gives me a proper kiss that lights a fire inside me and causes my knees to go weak. Out of breath, I place my hands on his chest and give him a playful shove. His arms reach out for me and I back up.

"You're not playing fair," I tell him.

He moves toward me, eyes twinkling with mischief. "I don't want to play fair."

I beg and plead, but he takes me in his arms and kisses me with such passion my head swims. At the last moment, just as I feel as if I'm lifting off like a rocket, Jared holds me at arm's length. "See what happens when I'm alone with you. I lose all control."

He releases me and I pick up a plate and walk to the stove. With a smile I say, "Well, then, maybe I should move in with Aunt Sarah and Uncle Frank until after we're married."

"Are you threatening me?" he asks.

"No, that isn't my intention. I thought it might be easier …"

Jared presses a finger over my mouth and turns serious. "I am not willing to spend one night without you under this roof, so get that notion out of your head."

He says this with such tenderness that my heart leaps for joy.

The following morning I arrive in the clinic to find Thad already in surgery. I put on a mask and gloves, don scrubs and back through the door leading into surgery room one where a border collie lies on a table sedated. Thad looks up. His eyes peer at me over the surgical mask.

"What's up?" I ask.

"His owner tied him in the back of the truck. There were a couple dogs on the side of the road and he jumped out. The rope was long enough for him to slip under the back tire. I'm amazed the only thing broken is his leg."

My eyes gravitate to the white bone protruding from the shaved area. "Do you need any help?"

"No, but there are a couple calls on the board; nothing serious, just a snotty nose and a stallion that needs suturing. Watch him. He's big and likes to bite. Sedate him real good before you try to sew him up."

With Thad's warning fresh on my mind, I decide to tackle the hard case first. When I arrive at the Thompson ranch, I ring the doorbell to the main house. A kind looking women in her late sixties directs me to a barn some hundred feet away. I get back in the truck and pull up to the building. The double doors in front are shut, so I get out and slide them open, making certain there is plenty of room inside for the truck. I drive in, turn the motor off and close the doors. Somewhere down the dark aisle I hear a voice.

"We're down here."

Thad wasn't kidding. A lone light hangs from the ceiling in the middle of the stall. Standing knee-deep in bedding is the biggest horse I've ever seen—most likely a Clydesdale. He's wearing a leather halter. The attached lead rope is tied to a sturdy ring mounted in the wall. The mammoth equine rolls his eyes at me and shows a lot of white as I walk up to him for a closer look at the open wound. His owner, Jack Thompson, is standing at the stallion's head. The rancher is six feet plus and weighs a good two-hundred pounds, but he's dwarfed by his horse.

My presence upsets the horse. He paws the straw and snorts, blowing mucus all over the front of Jack's jacket. The rancher looks down at the mess in disgust then slaps the horse on his muscled neck. "Knock it off Monty. She's here to help," he tells the ill-mannered beast. Then, looking me up and down, he says, "Where's Thad? He knows Monty better than anyone."

"In surgery, I'll have to do."

My gut doesn't believe I will do, but that doesn't matter. The patient is bleeding from a cut right above his knee joint.

"Do you have a twitch you can put on his nose to keep his attention off me while I give him a sedative?" I ask.

Jack nods. He produces a twitch made of steel and rope from the back pocket of his jeans. He must do this often because he grabs the horse's upper lip and slips the looped rope on and gives it a couple good twists. The big horse protests a bit, and Jack twists again. With the Stallion's attention off me, I tap the vein in the massive animal's neck to bring it to the surface and insert the needle. The stallion lifts his head and Jack hangs on to the twitch for dear life. If I wasn't so scared, I'd laugh. Jack's feet are dangling off the ground.

It isn't long before the sedative takes effect. The stallion's head drops, and Jack's feet hit the ground with a little thud. I examine the gash and determine this is a cosmetic matter. I shave the area around the wound, clean it with surgical scrub, and before the anesthetic wears off, I sew the three inch opening closed.

"You're going to have to keep a bandage on it, Jack. If he's a chewer, put hot sauce on the bandage to keep him from pulling it off. Works with most horses. Clean the wound every day and spray it with a topical antibiotic. You have one, don't you?"

The rancher grins. "Oh, yes. Monty gets into trouble on a regular basis, most of the time it's only nicks and scrapes. He just got a little rambunctious when I turned him out to play."

"Horses do that when they're confined for long periods of time," I say and leave the stall. Most ranchers don't balk at removing stitches which saves me a trip. "Are you okay with taking the sutures out?" I ask.

Jack removes the twitch and steps away from the stallion. "Not really. I'd rather pay you, if you don't mind."

I wait for him to close the stall door. "It won't be me. I'm getting married January 1st. Thad will do it. I'll make sure to put it in his appointment book."

The rancher walks me to my truck and waits while I dispose of the suture kit in the trash receptacle. I'm conscious of his stare as I write up his bill and hand it to him.

Jack stares at me for a couple seconds while rolling a toothpick back and forth between his lips. "Jared's a lucky man. A beautiful woman and a vet besides," he says. "Can't hurt to have a vet in the family, can it?"

Once I'm in the truck, I hang my head out and wink at him. "No, it sure can't. Do you suppose Brandon had that in mind when he sent me to vet school?"

The rancher's eyes twinkle. "On more than one occasion he expressed the hope that you and Jared would tie the knot.

Yep, I bet Brandon is right pleased with himself—putting you through veterinary school and all."

Jack ambles toward the double doors and opens them. As I drive through, he touches the brim of his worn Stetson.

My next patient is an old pony with a snotty nose. A quick examination confirms my thoughts. "His lungs are pretty bad," I tell the young girl holding the lead rope. She can't be more than fifteen.

Her eyes cloud over. "Do you think he'll make it?" she asks as I inject antibiotic into his thick neck muscle.

I rub the injection with my fingers to disburse the medicine and smile at her. "He'll be giving you trouble in no time."

She watches me grind up horse aspirin.

"What's that for?"

"Just a little something to bring his temperature down," I tell her while digging around in the drawer of the vet truck to find a large syringe. I cut the tip off, pour the powder in, add water and shake until the powder dissolves. Getting the pony to take the medicine is another matter. When I attempt to put the syringe in the corner of his mouth, he swings his head back and forth. After several tries, she says, "Here, let me try."

The pony not only allows her to dose him with the medicine, he licks his lips afterwards. With a shake of my head,

I return to my truck and retrieve two bottles of pills and count out forty more which I drop in a plastic bag. I hand the bottles and bag to her and she clutches them to her chest. Her bottom lips quivers so I pat her shoulder.

"Don't worry, I've seen worse. He should recover nicely. Grind up twelve pills morning and night for ten days and put the antibiotic in his grain if he refuses it orally, just like I did with the aspirin. Squirt it as far back in his mouth as you can." Tears fill her eyes. I bend down and reassure her with a smile. "Trust me. He will be okay in a week or two. Just follow my directions.

I make billing notations in my journal and open the door of my truck. Before getting in, I turn to her. "I want you to keep him inside. Make sure he has plenty of water and walk him ten minutes three times a day. His temperature will spike tonight, but it should go down within a couple of days; if it doesn't, call me."

As I drive away, I call back to her. "Tell your parents I'll bill them."

When I return to the clinic, Thad is with his patient who is now wearing a plaster cast and looking very sad from inside his large crate.

"How'd it go?" I ask while hanging my coat on the coat rack in the reception area.

"Good. I used a metal plate and screws." Thad looks me up and down and grins. "How was the stud horse? Did he try to eat you?" I ignore his teasing smile and the fact he's following me to the small kitchen.

He leans against the door and waits for me to pour a cup of coffee. I add cream and push past him, down the hall and into the tiny office. I make notes on my computer, add to his list of appointments removing the stud's stitches and then I kick back and stare at him.

"So, you haven't been around the house lately. Did Laura give you the boot?"

Color creeps up his neck, into his cheeks. I hit a nerve.

"Of course not, I don't want to get my hopes up and then have her go back to Romania. Is there anything wrong with that?"

I study him for several seconds over the rim of my cup. "I'm not buying it. You're afraid of getting too close to her. You're afraid she'll steal your heart and you might have to make a choice."

He shrugs and stalks off the way men do when they don't want to talk about it. I stare after Thad and grin. Methinks he protests too much, so I call after him. "That's the chicken's way out, Thad. She's a nice girl. Face it, you're attracted to her." Thad disappears into his office, but he doesn't close the door. Louder than necessary I add, "What does it matter if her roots are in Romania? If she feels the same way you do, she'll stay here. She doesn't have family back there. Remember."

Chapter 23

The house smells of pumpkin bread and sugar cookies, two of my favorites. Christmas carols add to the festive occasion. I hang up my coat and walk toward the sounds of laughter coming from the living room. Jared is standing before a blue spruce so tall it comes very close to touching the vaulted ceiling. I look around the room. Boxes of decorations are strewn about the floor and on the couch. Laura and Mom are sitting in arm chairs near the fireplace where logs burn brightly

"Hello. I'm home."

Jared spins around and his eyes brighten. He greets me with a kiss and draws me toward the warmth of the flames. "You're like an ice cube. I'll get you a cup of tea," he says on his way out of the room.

I stare after him in dismay. I can't recall when he went from a self-centered, womanizing man to this. I shake my head and smile at Laura, who is knitting a sweater in a delicate shade of pink. She cocks her head, as sightless people do. "How was your day, Kayla?"

"Yes, how was your day?" Mom echoes.

I expel a long, frustrated sigh. "Well, I wrangled with a stallion while attempting to sew him up, and I doctored a young girl's pony suffering from a terrible cold that might have turned into pneumonia if we were a day or two later. Then, I spent the rest of the day checking on our in-house patients. After that I caught up on paperwork. Just another day at the clinic," I reply with a chuckle.

Jared returns with a tray containing a tea pot, milk, sugar, four cups and saucers, which are stacked two on two, and a plate of sugar cookies. He sets the tray on the end table next to Mom's chair with nary a tinkle of china and pours tea.

Murmurs of, "Thank you," bring a smile to his face.

"So, how was your day?" he inquires.

Laughter breaks out, and he looks from one face to the other in confusion. "Did I say something funny?" he asks, arching an eyebrow.

Mom sips her tea and then explains. "Seems Laura and I asked that question while you were in the kitchen."

Jared turns to me. "And?"

I relate the story about the stallion and the pony in more detail. When I get to the size of the stallion and how he pushed me around and lifted Jack right off his feet, Jared bellows, "What's the matter with Thad anyway? He shouldn't be sending you out to take care of an animal that size!" At first I'm not too concerned but then Jared's face turns red with anger.

"He didn't have a choice. Thad was in the middle of surgery when the call came in. Besides, I've handled much worse."

Jared slams his tea cup down and turns toward the telephone. "I'll have a word with him." The old Jared rushes back. "No way will I allow my wife to work under those conditions."

Within seconds we are arguing like old times. He stops to take a breath and I say, "Just because we are getting married doesn't mean you control me. I'm a grown woman, and I can take care of myself." The words explode from my mouth in the heat of anger. When I realize what I've done, I look around the room. Mom is speechless. Laura is trying her best to hide her embarrassment. Rather than spar with Jared over something so stupid, I leave the room and go upstairs.

Later, after a quiet dinner with stilted conversation, I apologize to Mom and Laura.

"It's over. Let's pretend it didn't happen," Mom says.

Laura remains quiet. I'm sure she feels out of place.

Jared clears his throat. "That goes for me too."

Mom pushes her chair back and comes around the table. She hugs Jared and moves on to me. As her arms tighten around me, she whispers in my ear. "He's a work in progress. We all are."

She takes Laura's hand and explains that there is a Christmas program starting in a few minutes. "Laura and I have been looking forward to it," she says as the two of them leave the room.

Their departure leaves an uncomfortable silence. I'm about to say something to ease the tension when Jared pushes his chair away from the table.

Great, he's going to leave me sitting here.

To my surprise, he stops and kneels beside my chair. The stubborn cut of his jaw softens as he reaches for my hand. Seeing him like this brings tears to my eyes.

"I'm sorry, Kayla. It's just that I love you so much."

I bite my bottom lip to stop it from trembling and look down. His eyes plead with me to forgive him long before he asks.

"It's no excuse, I know that. Please, forgive me."

My head nods of its own accord. Seconds later, I'm in his arms. He kisses me, and when our lips part, he says, "I promise not to interfere with your career if you promise to stand up for yourself with Thad. He hired you as a surgeon. Now he's sending you out on farm calls."

"But the practice is growing so fast…"

"He can hire another vet." The words slip out and Jared grins. "Sorry, I just broke my promise, didn't I?"

"Not really. You're entitled to your opinion."

I begin to clear the table, and he joins in the task. Once the dishwasher is loaded, we make our way to the living room and the undecorated tree. Later, when Mom and Laura join us, Jared is wearing more tinsel than the tree.

Laura returns to her chair and takes up her knitting. Mom sits back and motions to bare spots on the tree. By ten o'clock Jared and I stand back to admire our handiwork.

"Perfect," he announces. He turns to Mom and says, "Maggie, will you do the honor of plugging in the lights."

"Absolutely beautiful," I whisper when the tree lights come on.

Mom reads the Christmas story from the Bible. After the last verse, Jared plugs in the cord that lights the star atop the tree. In year's past it had been Brandon's job to end the tree-lighting ceremony by saying, "This star represents the birth of the Christ child, the light of the world." Tonight Jared takes on the role of head of household. In an emotion filled moment he speaks the familiar words and the most wonderful thing happens. From the stereo in the other room comes a chorus of beautiful voices singing *Silent Night, Holy Night.*

"What a perfect ending to a beautiful day," I murmur and smile up at him. My happiness is short lived when my cell phone rings. "Not tonight," I groan.

Thad's number appears on the lighted screen. With a sigh of resignation I flip open my phone.

"What's up Thad?"

"Kayla, I hate to spoil your evening but I need your help in surgery. One of Harold Jensen's boarder collies is in bad shape."

Jared helps me into my coat then insists on driving me to the clinic. Twenty minutes later he pulls up to the back entrance. Without a word, we hurry to the door. I have a moment of trouble but eventually insert the key in the lock. Jared makes his way to reception area in the front of the building and I go to the sink to scrub. When I join Thad in surgery, he looks up from his patient, who is a mass of open wounds.

"What have we got?" I ask.

Thad's voice is muffled by his surgical mask. Nonetheless, I get the message.

"It appears he was drug quite a distance by his leash without the driver's knowledge."

I glance from the patient to Thad. He reads the question in my eyes.

"Harold tied the dog to the bumper of his truck to allow him to do his duty. He went inside to wait and his wife called to him from the kitchen. Harold went to see what she needed. In the meantime, their son decided to go into town to meet his girlfriend when she got off work. He didn't see the dog tied to the truck in the dark."

"So, he drove off dragging the dog?"

"Yes. He'd be dead except Jensen's son heard a thump about a mile or so down the road and stopped to see what the problem was."

The dog's respirations are shallow. An I.V. hangs from the ceiling. Taking care not to do further damage, we roll the dog over. I'm taken by surprise at what I see. The dog's eye is out of the socket like some grotesque cartoon character. I examine it and find no damage to the eye itself.

"He must have hit the road pretty hard to do this," I tell Thad.

Thad nods and waits for me to cleanse the area. We agree to put the eye back and sew the lid shut for a few days to give it time to heal. This is done with little trouble even though we don't know if the dog will be able to see out of it. Time will tell. X-rays show broken ribs but no internal damage of consequence, hard to believe under the circumstances. Several large gashes need sutures. I shave the areas and begin this process while Thad studies the x-rays of the dog's hind legs.

"Multiple fractures, his leash must have gotten tangled up in the back tire," Thad says while laying out the necessary equipment and supplies to fix the fractures.

"That much damage to the eye also means he's got a concussion," I say, looking up from my work.

"Yes. The next twenty-four hours will be critical. While you finish up, I'll call Dana and have her come in to keep an eye on him."

The door closes with a swish. Five minutes later, Thad returns. He adjusts the I.V. that administers the sedative and we begin surgery on the dog's hind legs. The next time I glance at the clock it's after midnight. My back aches as I straighten up. By the time Dana arrives, the dog is in recovery. She greets us with a sleepy smile and reads the chart.

Now that she is here, I take my leave. While washing up, I glance in the mirror and wince. My blood-splattered surgical gown makes it look as if I've been to war. Tired eyes stare back at me. I drop the gown in the dirty laundry bin on the way out and find Jared asleep on the couch. I nudge him, and his eyes blink open. It takes a moment, but he finally sits up.

"How's the dog?" he asks in a sleepy voice.

"We won't know much until tomorrow. He's in pretty bad shape. We'll have to wait and see what happens. The next twenty-four hours will be critical.

"Are you sure you should leave?" he asks.

Nodding, I reach for my jacket. "Thad called Dana. She'll stay with him tonight. He's in good hands in more ways than one." I tuck my arm in Jared's and pull him toward the door. "Thanks for coming with me, I appreciate it."

He kisses the tip of my nose and smiles. "My pleasure, ma'am. Anytime."

Christmas arrives in snowy splendor.

Aunt Sarah, Uncle Frank and Rebecca arrive. Behind them is Thad bearing an armful of gifts. I hide my surprise and welcome him. Somewhere behind me Mom calls out,

"Thaddeus, I'm so glad you could join us. Laura will be pleased."

At least he didn't show up on our doorstep uninvited, I tell myself. Then I'm ashamed I didn't invite him myself. I relieve him of a few packages and usher him into the living room where Rebecca waits anxiously by the tree. When she can stand it no longer, she says, "Are we ready to open gifts?"

Laughter rings out and her young face turns red.

"Of course, Sweetheart," Mom says. She turns to Jared. "Will you play Santa?"

I see a hint of sadness in her eyes as Jared takes his father's place by the mound of packages. We wait in anticipation as he hunts for the first present. When he finds it, he holds it up for everyone to see. "This one is for Laura." He passes the package to me to give to Laura, and her face glows.

As she tears away the wrapping, I thank God for allowing me to see Christmas through Laura's sightless eyes. Laura doesn't dwell on the materialistic side of Christmas. Instead, she holds on to the real meaning of Christmas— Christ's birth in Bethlehem and the promise of all that comes with that birth.

The package is from Thad. Laura's fingers caress the silky scarf she holds to her cheek. "Thank you, Thad. I'll wear it often."

"It's a beautiful shade of red," Mom explains.

"Red is one of my favorite colors," Laura says.

"This one is for Kayla from Laura." Jared hands me a beautiful, pink foil wrapped package with a lovely silver bow adorned with a piece of mistletoe.

I open the package and gasp with surprise. A pink sweater—not just any sweater, but the sweater Laura spent hours kitting. How many times had I wondered who would wear such a loving gift?

Stepping over paper and ribbons, I wrap Laura in a warm embrace. In those seconds I recall my feelings of resentment and jealousy toward her. The moment is a humbling experience I won't forget.

"Thank you so much. It's beautiful. Every time I wear it, I'll think of you." I give her a final little squeeze and return to my seat.

The next packages are Rebecca's gifts to Aunt Sarah and Uncle Frank. Rebecca sits up and chews on her fingernails in anticipation as a myriad of thoughts pass across her young face. In the end she has nothing to worry about. Her choice brings a squeal of delight from Aunt Sarah and, "What a thoughtful gift," from Uncle Frank.

Jared smiles at me from across the mound of Christmas wrapping. He's wearing my Christmas present to him—a new jacket with the McChesney logo on the back. As if to thank him again, I touch the diamond earrings I'm wearing.

"I love them. Thank you."

"And I love you," he says.

My heart flutters at the ease with which he says this.

I look around the room. No one seems to notice our tender moment. Thad is sitting on the arm of Laura's chair. They look so comfortable together. Mom and Aunt Sarah are deep in conversation. Rebecca is holding up a skirt and sweater, a gift from Mom. Beside her are several albums of Christian rock, all on her Christmas wish list.

The clock chimes one. Mom, Aunt Sarah and I leave the others to clean up the mess. It is my job to set the dining room table while Mom and Aunt Sarah go to the kitchen. Twenty minutes later Mom brings in a standing rib roast which she sets near the end of the table where Jared will do the carving. Aunt Sarah and I make several trips to and from the kitchen. On our last trip, I poke my head into the living room.

Five anxious faces look my way when they hear me say, "Dinner is served."

Once we are seated, Jared asks Uncle Frank to say grace. Uncle Frank is a simple man. He talks to God as if He is in the room.

"Heavenly Father, we are grateful for the blessings bestowed upon us all year, but we are especially thankful today as you remind us what Christmas is all about. It's your Son's birthday. He's the reason for the season. Not the presents."

And everyone says, "Amen."

J. B. Williams

Chapter 24

Dad and my stepmother, Joyce, arrive the day after Christmas. They greet Mom with a hug and a kiss, and then they tell each other how good the other one looks. Laura stands to one side wearing a quizzical expression. I'm sure she's as amazed at this unusual relationship as many others have been in the past when they find out Mom and Dad were once married to each other. As usual, Mom insists Joyce and Dad stay with us, which always displaces Jared from his bedroom. This time he doesn't mind. He insists on sleeping in the bunk house.

"Oh, we can't have you doing that," Dad says.

"Of course you can," Jared replies. He winks at me and adds, "Stay as long as you like."

The phone rings, and I excuse myself to answer it. On the other end is a familiar voice.

"Hi, bride to be," Clara says.

"You're here," I say.

"We got in late last night."

"How was your flight?"

"Crowded, every seat was taken. Enough of that, let's talk about the wedding. I'll bet you're a bundle of nerves."

"I am. Mom and Dad just arrived. When the phone rang, I thought it might be Derek."

"What's he been up to?" Clara asks.

I think back and recall the exact day…almost to the hour. "That would be when he left for seminary. I can't wait to see him."

"You're not going to believe this, but he's married."

"What!" Clara wails. "No way."

"That's what I said. He met her in Tennessee. She is a widow with a young daughter. To hear him tell it, he fell head over heels for her. They were married a month after they met. He attends seminary and is the Youth Minister of the church they attend. His wife is Director of Music."

Clara sighs heavily for effect. "How romantic is that?"

"Something to tell their kids about," I reply.

"Didn't Derek have a son? Or am I dreaming?" Clara asks.

"Yes, he's twelve."

Clara groans with despair. "Time flies. Doesn't it?"

"It does. Speaking of time, I have to go. We'll talk tomorrow. Bring the dress. I'm dying to see it."

We say goodbye and I join the others in the living room. Mom, Joyce and Laura are sitting on the couch. Dad and Jared are standing in front of the fire with their backs to the warmth. Dad looks wonderful. He's a little heavier than a year ago with more gray in his hair, but the changes give him an air of elegance. I can't help but wonder about Joyce. She never changes, except for her hair, which is strawberry blond this year. Her caring nature endears her to everyone she meets. Laura is no exception.

Dad hurries to greet me. "Well, here's the bride now. I didn't get a chance to tell you how beautiful you are, Princess."

I hate the nickname, but it's stuck with me over the years and as long as he is the only one who uses it, I won't complain. Dad takes my arm and leads me to Jared, who bends to give me a kiss.

"Who was that?" he asks.

"Clara."

"Did you speak with Bryan?" Jared asks.

"No, I didn't. They'll be here tomorrow."

Dad stands before us grinning. It's like someone painted the smile on his face. Even when he speaks, it's there. "I knew you guys would find each other," he says.

From the couch Joyce adds, "Your father is an old romantic. He cried like a baby when you called to tell us you were engaged."

The doorbell rings. On his way to answer it, Jared says, "I wonder who that can be."

I can tell he already knows. From the hallway, Jared's voice rings out. "Derek, come on in. And who are these folks?"

Derek looks wonderful, as handsome as ever. I bet the females in his congregation swoon each time he stands behind the lectern. The little girl is absolutely gorgeous. She has her mother's beautiful blue eyes and petite frame. Derek's wife is small, five feet, with sandy blond hair, blues eyes and a ready smile.

Derek walks toward me and wraps me in his arms and holds me tight while kissing the side of my face. Over his shoulder I see Jared and Derek's wife smiling at us. When Derek releases me, he extends a hand to his bride.

"Kayla, I'd like you to meet Stephanie and our daughter, Rosemary."

Rosemary isn't shy at all. She wriggles in her mother's arms and begs to get down. As soon as she's on the floor, Rosemary goes from one outstretched hand to the other while her mother and I get acquainted. Within minutes, Stephanie and I are reminiscing about the time Derek and I spent traveling the rodeo circuit.

"He was a great trainer and teacher," I tell her, looking over my shoulder at Derek who is talking with Jared.

"Derek loves you very much," Stephanie says without a hint of jealousy. "He talks about you all the time...especially to the kids at church. He uses you as an example of how God works things out in our lives if we ask Him to."

This takes me by surprise. I'm not sure I want to be used as an example. My life so far hasn't been what I'd call a pillar of faith and good works. When I voice this concern to Stephanie, she smiles. "Life dealt you some bad blows, but you took them on the chin. You didn't lose faith, Kayla. According to Derek, you asked God to give your life purpose after learning your barrel racing days were over. I'm certain it was God's plan for you to choose veterinary medicine."

Looking back, I know she's right and I tell her so.

"I hear that you're the director of music at Derek's church."

Stephanie's face brightens even more, if that's possible. "Yes. Like you, God has a plan for me. I was in my last year of college when my husband died in a car accident. I didn't think I'd ever marry again and then I met Derek. It happened so fast. Six weeks later we were married."

Stephanie turns to look at Derek. As if he feels her stare, he glances over at us and smiles. Her eyes never leave his face. "I don't believe in coincidences, Kayla. Not where God is concerned."

The statement is simple, yet profound. I am pondering the wisdom of it when Mom's laughter rings out. Stephanie and I look over our shoulders. Rosemary is sitting on Mom's lap reading from a book she holds upside down.

A thought comes to me and I turn to Stephanie. "Do you think Rosemary would like to have a part in the wedding?"

Stephanie's gaze goes back to her animated daughter. "Are you sure? She's a handful."

"Positive. I've always dreamed of having a flower girl sprinkle rose petals at my wedding. I know it's silly, but I saw it in a movie."

Stephanie's eyes brighten and she laughs. "Why not, but remember I warned you."

Bryan and Clara come over the next morning. Other than looking a tad tired, they look marvelous. I'm glad that Joyce and Dad are visiting friends. This gives Clara and me time to play catch up while Jared and Bryan sit back and listen. It isn't long before our girl talk bores them. They excuse themselves to watch football in the den. Once they are gone, I close the door and we get down to business.

"Where are the kids?" I ask.

"We couldn't pry them away from the television." Clara wrinkles her nose in disgust. "Just wait until you have kids. They are either in school, in front of the television or sleeping. Bryan and I hound them to exercise their imagination by writing or drawing, but it's useless."

I sympathize with a smile and suggest Clara show me her dress. When I learn she designed it herself, I am impressed.

"I didn't know you do that!"

She waves off my adulation. "It's a hobby. I'm not good enough to have a line of my own, one day maybe."

I examine the dress and look up at her with wide-eyed wonder. "It's beautiful and made with such care. Clara, you should at least give it a try. You already have a clientele since you work on Broadway."

I draw the drapes and help Clara into her dress. "Perfect. Absolutely perfect," I breathe out. I'm about to tell her if I had her talent I'd have my own clothing line when the doorbell rings.

Moment's later Mom ushers Mrs. Cummings in. The elderly woman bubbles over with excitement. "As promised, your gown is ready." She opens the box and with tender, loving care hands me my wedding dress.

With a gasp, Mom hurries to close the door. She turns and leans against it. "Ladies, we have to be careful. We can't have the bridegroom sneaking a look, now can we?" When she catches her breath, she insists I try the dress on in case further adjustments are necessary.

"Yes, put it on, Kayla," Clara urges.

Mrs. Cummings sits in an arm chair and waits patiently as I slip out of my sweater and slacks and into my mother's wedding dress. Now I know how Cinderella felt. I marvel at the transformation as I stare at myself in the mirror. Behind me, Mom is in tears. From across the room, Mrs. Cummings says, "Somewhere in the box is a head piece and veil." Her plump face creases into a smile. "It's something new...from me."

Clara's skirt rustles as she hurries across the carpet. I watch her lift a beaded head piece with a long veil from beneath a layer of tissue paper. She places it on my head and my heart flutters. Instead of Mom crying alone, I burst into tears of happiness.

"Oh, you mustn't cry," Mrs. Cummings says as she struggles to her feet and hurries across the room to dry my eyes. "We don't want stains on the dress, now do we?"

Mrs. Cummings turns me around several times and nods her approval. Once the inspection is over, she insists I take the dress off before I get it dirty. Clara and I muffle our laughter, and I do as she says. While I pull on my clothes, Mom hangs the dress on a hanger, slips protective plastic over it and whisks it away just as Jared and Bryan walk in.

"I guess we're too late," Bryan says.

"Seems so," Jared responds.

"Late for what?" Mom asks.

"To see the dress," Jared replies.

Mom wags a finger at him while attempting to keep a straight face. "It is bad luck for the groom to see the bride in her dress before the wedding. You should be ashamed of yourself for trying to sneak a peek."

It's all in good fun, Jared teasing Mom and her scolding him. Everyone has a good laugh then Mom suggests tea in the living room. She disappears out the door and rejoins us ten minutes later carrying a large tray of cups, saucers, milk, and a plate of sugar cookies and pumpkin bread. Mom pours a cup for

Mrs. Cummings and takes it to her. Then she serves the rest of us. The cookies and bread disappears quickly. With nothing left to eat, Jared suggests we adjourn to the kitchen to raid the refrigerator.

Mrs. Cummings declines the offer, so Mom sees her out while the rest of us, including Laura, make our way toward the kitchen. By the time Mom arrives, Jared and I are making sandwiches from the left-over roast beef. Bryan and Clara are sitting at the table visiting with Laura, who is regaling them with vivid descriptions of the living conditions in the Romanian orphanages. By the time the sandwiches are ready, Bryan and Clara are pledging money for the orphanage where Laura grew up.

Jared leans into me and whispers in my ear. "And you were worried that Laura might feel left out."

The way he smiles at me makes me feel like the luckiest woman alive.

Chapter 25

December 31st.

Rather than join Clara, Bryan and a few friends, Jared and I spend the evening with the family. Derek and Stephanie declined our invitation to join us because they agreed to chaperone the New Year's Eve party for the teenagers of our church. It is with some reluctance that Uncle Frank agrees to allow Rebecca to attend these festivities, and then only because Derek promises to keep an eye on her.

The doorbell rings. Jared answers it and brings Derek and Stephanie into the living room. Rebecca bounds to her feet, anxious to leave before Uncle Frank embarrasses her with last minute instructions on how to behave. I fear growing up is not going to be easy for her. I envision Uncle Frank following her on her first date. Yet, the fact he loves her so much warms my heart. Kids around the world should be so fortunate.

Derek and Stephanie stay long enough for a glass of cider. Then they are off. I'm amazed Rosemary doesn't seem to mind that her parents left without her. Within minutes, she is standing on the coffee table regaling us with her version of Mary Had A Little Lamb, over and over again. I see by his smile that Jared is under her spell. If one of us makes an attempt to leave the room, Rosemary stands with her hands on her hips and calls us back.

The production goes on until Mom announces she's going to the kitchen to make hot chocolate. Rosemary jumps off the table with a thud and follows. In her absence, Jared claps his hands and has a good chuckle.

"I'd like a half-dozen like her," he says.

I'm speechless. To tell you the truth, we haven't discussed the size family we want. I assumed two would be sufficient.

There's a round of laughter after his announcement; mine a little more hesitant than the others. I find it rather difficult to see myself mothering six children. I'm not sure I'm capable of doing a good job with one. Rather than spoil the fun, I feign a smile.

"I wouldn't mind," Dad says.

Joyce agrees. "We love the grandchildren we have, the more the better."

Dad and Joyce are special. They make no distinction between children, step-children, grandchildren or step-grandchildren.

Everyone stops talking when Mom returns. She cocks her head and gives us a bewildered stare. "What's better?"

"Lots of grandchildren," Joyce replies.

Mom rolls her eyes and looks to me for an explanation. When I give her none, she tosses me a look that says `we'll talk about this later'.

Rosemary stands beside Mom. She's wearing one of Mom's aprons. Her tiny shoes are barely visible beneath the fabric. I'm not the only one who thinks this is a moment for posterity. Jared springs to his feet. On the way out of the room, he says, "Don't either of you move. I'm getting my camera." He darts from the room and returns with his digital camera. As instructed, Mom and Rosemary wait. When Jared returns, Rosemary obliges him by posing with her small tray of cookies and breads. Her little face glows with pride in the firelight as she carries the tray around the room. Alas, being an entertainer and hostess takes its toll. As soon as the tray is empty, she curls up on the couch and falls asleep. She's not the only one who is tired. By eleven o'clock I'm yawning. Rather than join the others in a rousing game of charades, I sit beside Laura and stretch my shoeless feet toward the fire.

For a while we enjoy the quiet. And then Laura turns to me. "This time tomorrow you'll be a married woman."

Her observation sends little goose bumps up and down my arms. With a sigh, I reply, "So I will. It doesn't seem possible."

Laura slants her head and listens to the rambunctious behavior across the room. She smiles and says, "They're having fun. I like it when people laugh. Sometimes at the orphanage I didn't laugh for a long time."

I study her profile in the firelight and try to imagine her life as a young child. I contrast her growing up years to Rosemary, who is sleeping with her cheek resting on her tiny hands. I watch her breathe and decide she doesn't have a care in the world.

I return my gaze to Laura. "If the memories are so awful, why do you want to go back? I know Mom would love it if you decided to make your home here. The house is going to be empty without Jared and me."

She ponders that thought. "You'll only be gone for two weeks."

"No, Laura, Jared and I won't be living in this house. We're moving into the guest house. I thought I told you." I see by her face further explanation is needed. "Jared and I have a lot to work through. It's better if we do it alone."

I see that something is bothering her. "What is it, Laura?"

"I thought maybe you didn't want to live here because of me." Her lip quivers.

I slip out of my chair and draw her into my arms. "No, silly girl, I love you. Jared loves you. It will break our hearts if you leave." In an attempt to convince her further I add, "You are like a sister to me." I press a wet cheek against hers and whisper, "Stay, Laura. There's nothing keeping you in Romania. You don't have to live there to help."

Laura brushes a hand over her cheek and manages a smile. "I will think about it," she says just as the doorbell rings. Voices in the hallway quickly draw her attention away from our conversation. She recognizes one voice in particular and her face radiates happiness.

"Thaddeus," Mom calls out. "Come and play charades with us."

"Later, Maggie." Thad walks over to us and squats beside Laura. He lays his hand on hers. "I came to wish you a Happy New Year. If I'm lucky, my pager won't go off."

Like Stephanie said, 'Coincidence is not in God's vocabulary'. Thad may not know it yet, but there is another wedding in the future.

Twenty minutes before twelve everyone puts on silly hats. Mom passes out horns and rattles. The clock strikes twelve. The noise is deafening, yet Rosemary sleeps through the merriment. Jared seeks me out and draws me close. As our lips meet, he reminds me what tomorrow brings.

"You'll be mine," he whispers. "And I promise you a honeymoon neither of us will forget."

Fireworks explode on the television screen. Times Square erupts into pandemonium. Joyce and Mom dart out of the room and return with champagne. Holding his glass high, Uncle Frank yells, "Happy New Year everyone."

From the corner of my eye, I see Thad kiss Laura. If he hasn't figured it out yet, he will. She's in love with him. And he's in love with her.

Once the excitement and well wishes die down, I excuse myself. "If you all don't mind, I'm going to bed. A bride with dark circles under her eyes is not a pretty picture."

Dad sets his glass down on the coffee table and strides across the room. He kisses me and blubbers something about losing his daughter. If this is what one glass of champagne does to him, I'll see that he drinks apple cider tomorrow. Joyce hugs me close and tells me to sleep well. Mom, Aunt Sarah and Uncle Frank do the same, minus the sleep well part. They know me too well. Nothing bothers my sleep.

Jared kisses me one last time. He waits at the bottom of the stairs until I wave from the landing and then he goes to the closet to get his jacket. From there he blows me a kiss and disappears into the night followed by Thad who has agreed to keep him company in the bunkhouse tonight.

The next day a tap at the door awakens me. I open my eyes and notice that the sun is shining, a rarity this time of year. I plump my pillow and put it behind me just as Mom pokes her head into the room.

"Is the bride ready for breakfast?"

The mere mention of food makes my stomach growl.

"I'm starved."

To my delight, Mom brings enough food for both of us. She sets a cup of coffee and a glass of orange juice on the nightstand and offers me a plate piled high with an omelet. She settles herself in the chair near the window and for the longest time she stares at me. It's as if she's remembering every facet of my life up until this moment. And then she says, "I can't believe my little girl is getting married."

Tears fill her eyes. She wipes them away with her napkin and picks up her fork. We eat in silence, content to have this quiet time together. Like so many young women, I dreamed of my wedding morning and what it would be like. I envisioned Mom giving me words of wisdom from her years of experience and later the excitement of having friends help me dress. We would laugh and cry and act silly in an effort to calm my nerves.

Then Dad would come for me.

"Are you nervous?" Mom asks.

Her voice brings me back. I look at her and nod.

"That's normal. I remember…" She bites her lip and begins again. "I was so nervous when your father and I got married that I forgot my vows. Thank goodness I wrote them on a piece of paper and stuffed them inside my glove. But that won't happen to you."

The thought of forgetting the vows I wrote sends me into a panic.

"Are you sure? What if I do? What if I look up at Jared and my mind goes blank?"

Mom gives me a confident smile. "You won't forget. Trust me."

I'm not so sure. I set my half-eaten breakfast on the nightstand and reach for the glass of orange juice. I lean back against the headboard, close my eyes and listen to the voices in the lower part of the house.

"Must be the caterers," I muse aloud.

Mom agrees with a nod.

Butterflies dance in my stomach. I assure myself this is normal—that people get married every day and live to tell the story to their grandchildren. Nonetheless, my throat goes dry. I take a drink and will my nerves to go away. The next voice I hear is Clara calling my name from outside my bedroom door.

"Come in."

Clara bursts through the door and stops at the foot of my bed. Her hair is done up in a French twist fastened by a chic comb. She holds up something that looks like a brief case and smiles.

"I have in here the tools of my trade. So, get out of bed, take a shower and let's get to it, girl." Without warning, she yanks the covers away from me and hurries me off to the bathroom. Several minutes later, I return with a towel wrapped around my head. She pushes me into a chair and whips out her hair dryer while Mom clears away the breakfast dishes.

"If you girls don't need me, I'll see if Jared is up," she says and closes the door behind her.

Jared. I haven't thought about him all morning. Why is that? I decide it's because I'm too wrapped up in myself to consider he might be suffering from a case of pre-marital jitters too. I'm about to voice my concern to Clara when my cell phone rings. The first thought to cross my mind is that there is an emergency at the clinic. Then I remember Thad hired another vet in anticipation of me being gone for two weeks.

Clara retrieves the phone from my purse and hands it to me.

The voice on the other end sends a trickle of pleasure down my spine. "Good morning, beautiful. I just called to say I love you."

"I love you too."

"So, what are you doing?" he asks.

In the background I hear Thad. "Her bag is packed and she's getting ready to jump out the window."

"Tell Thaddeus I'll do anything to get out of work— even if that means going through with this wedding." I laugh to make sure Jared knows I'm teasing.

Jared repeats what I said to Thad and Thad howls with laughter.

"I'll see you in the living room. Don't be late," Jared says.

I wait for him to hang up before snapping my phone shut. The butterflies are gone, thanks to Jared. With a sigh, I gaze into the mirror and smile at Clara who is busy teasing my auburn tresses. She creates something simple, yet elegant. While combing the last hair in place, she asks, "Do you like it?"

"I love it. Thank you so much."

She stands back to evaluate the upswept hairdo and nods her approval.

"And now for your makeup."

She cleans my face, applies an astringent, moisturizing cream and foundation. Color is brushed into my cheeks. She outlines my lips and applies lipstick. I marvel at how steady her hand is as she applies eye shadow and liner and then the final touch, mascara, in several layers.

"What do you think?" she asks.

I can't speak. But Mom does when she enters the room. "Sweetheart, you're beautiful," she says. The words barely leave her mouth before she's stumbling over an explanation. "Not that you aren't beautiful every day—it's—well, today you're radiant."

"Clara is a miracle worker," I say.

Clara disagrees with a shake of her head. "You can't make a silk purse out of a sow's ear." She grins and adds,

"Cute, huh? But I can't take credit for that witty remark. Grandma used to say it all the time."

The rest of the morning is a blur, so much so, that I don't recall Joyce, Aunt Sarah and Rebecca joining us. Rebecca is stunning. I can't take my eyes off her. She looks so grown up in her ankle length dress and high heels. Her face glows with no tell tale signs of the late night New Year's Eve bash.

"You look beautiful, Rebecca."

"Thanks, Kayla. So do you."

Joyce rushes toward me with the intention of giving me a hug. Clara jumps between us which causes Joyce to stop. An awkward moment ensues while Joyce decides whether to be annoyed or laugh. Her good nature wins out. She hugs the next available person, which happens to be Mom. I watch them in the mirror while Mrs. Cummings fusses over last minute details to the gown. My attention is drawn away from Joyce and Mom when the door opens. Much ado is made over Rosemary when Stephanie brings her into the room. The little girl is a vision in a plum colored dress and black patent leather shoes. She is wearing the flower headpiece I ordered. Mom leaves Joyce and greets the two of them. She kneels in front of Rosemary and hands her the wicker basket filled with rose petals.

"When the music starts, you will sprinkle rose petals on the red carpet. Okay?"

Rosemary nods, but her attention is on me. She comes toward me, her blue eyes widening with wonder. "You look like a fairy godmother."

The room erupts into laughter. When it dies down, Mom attempts to continue her conversation with Rosemary. In an effort to make certain Rosemary doesn't stray off the red carpet, Mom motions for Rebecca to join them.

"Rosemary, this is my niece, Rebecca. She's going to be in the wedding too. Rebecca will walk right behind you. Okay?"

Rosemary nods and reaches into the basket. She takes out one rose petal and holds it very close to Mom's face. "See, I know what one is."

Everyone laughs, all except Mrs. Cummings, who has been having a bit of trouble securing the bridal veil. "Hold still," she commands. Behind me, Clara stifles a smile.

"There, that does it." Mrs. Cummings breathes a sigh of relief. "Stand up, let's have a look at you."

I do as I'm told and turn around several times. The verdict is unanimous. Murmurs of, "Beautiful, stunning, and perfect," pass around the room.

I'm not sure who suggests I walk to the window and back to make sure I can walk in the gown. I do as I'm told and stop to look down. The driveway is lined with cars. A moment of doubt strikes my heart, but when I turn around my apprehension is swept away by the look on Mom's face. She floats across the room and takes my hands in hers. Tears gather in her eyes, but she holds them back.

I wait for her last piece of advice, and she doesn't fail me.

"Tomorrow this day will be a beautiful memory. Try to remember each detail."

I'm speechless with emotion. I look around the room, and when I find my voice, which is a bit uncertain much like my legs, I say, "I love you all. Thank you so much for making this day special."

The knock at the door makes my heart races.

"Enter," Mom calls out.

Dad walks in and my dream becomes reality. He stares at me with tears in his eyes. I walk toward him and take his arm.

"You look beautiful," he whispers.

"And you look very handsome."

He kisses my cheek, and we watch Stephanie hurry Rosemary out of the room. Rebecca follows them. Aunt Sarah and Joyce wish me well and leave. Mom lingers a moment, touches my cheek and walks out of the room.

"Well, Sweetheart, I wish I had some words of wisdom for you. But I don't. Just be happy. And remember, no going to bed angry. That's something your Mom and I forgot. But it's good advice."

The harpist begins to play and the music wafts its way upstairs.

Clara brushes her cheek to mine, careful not to smudge my makeup. With a swish of satin she walks out the door and down the hallway. Dad and I follow. We stand at the top of the stairs until Clara reaches the foyer.

Dad squeezes my hand. "Well, this is it, Princess, are you ready?"

I nod and we descend the staircase. When we reach the bottom step, Stephanie sends Rosemary between the rows of chairs and then hurries along the outside of the chairs so she can meet her daughter near the front row. My fear that Rosemary won't follow directions is unfounded. She sprinkles petals, one by one, along the red carpet. Rebecca follows her, and I breathe a sigh of relief knowing Rosemary has someone to encourage her along in case she stops to speak to one of the guests, something I envision her doing. But Rosemary doesn't stop. She sprinkles the last rose petal and runs into her mother's arms.

Clara looks at me one last time and takes her husband's arm. They walk toward Jared and the minister.

When the bridal march begins, I seek Jared's face. Our eyes remain locked as Dad walks me toward him; every step makes my heart beat faster. I feel lightheaded, even a bit dizzy as Dad and I stop next to Jared.

"Who gives this woman in marriage?" the minister asks.

My parents answer in unison, "We do."

Dad kisses my cheek and hands me over to Jared. There's no going back now. In a few minutes Jared and I will be together forever. The thought overwhelms me, yet I have no doubt that God ordained this marriage long ago. The fear of forgetting my vows is replaced with unspeakable love as I listen to Jared. In his eyes I see the promise of long-lasting love.

"With this ring I thee wed," he says, slipping the ring on my finger.

I catch a glimpse of Mom, eyes bright with tears of happiness. She knew all along this day would come. So did Brandon.

When my turn comes, I say the words every bride longs to say to the man she will spend the rest of her life with. As I slide the simple band of gold on my beloved's finger, I can't help but think Brandon is nearby smiling his approval.

Other books in the series

Summer of Awakening

Chase Your Dreams

Note from the author:

It is my sincere hope that you enjoyed this three-book series for young Christian women. I pray that in some small way these stories communicated to you the importance of asking Jesus Christ to be the master of your life

I am available through my web site at www.janicebraunwilliams.com if you have any comments about this book or desire to learn more about the Christian faith.